3800 16 0002433 9

HIGH LIFE

D0487448

HIGHLAND
LIBRARIES

WITHDRAWN

Outlaw Express

Sheriff Alec Lawson had never robbed a train before. He'd infiltrated a band of outlaws to help capture them, but when they kidnapped Lacey Fry from the Leadville express, he had no choice but to try and rescue the young woman alone. Alec Lawson didn't know the territory and he didn't know the girl. He had to fight his way through the snowy mountains, trying to stay one step ahead of the pursuing outlaws.

Bill Alcott, the gang's leader, felt he had been fooled and then betrayed by Lawson, He had to kill him to avenge his brother and keep the respect of his men.

Lacey Fry had to ride as she'd never ridden before, and travel with a man she didn't know, who was her only hope of escaping a fate worse than death.

So the chase was on, through snow and bloodshed, until one of them could run no further and hunter and hunted finally came face to face.

Outlaw Express

Gillian F. Taylor

HIGHLAND
LIBRARIES

A Black Horse Western

ROBERT HALE

© Gillian F. Taylor 2017
First published in Great Britain 2017

ISBN 978-0-7198-2129-5

The Crowood Press
The Stable Block
Crowood Lane
Ramsbury
Marlborough
Wiltshire SN8 2HR

www.bhwesterns.com

Robert Hale is an imprint
of The Crowood Press

The right of Gillian F. Taylor to be identified as
author of this work has been asserted by her
in accordance with the Copyright, Designs and
Patents Act 1988

Typeset by
Derek Doyle & Associates, Shaw Heath
Printed and bound in Great Britain by
CPI Group (UK) Ltd, Croydon, CR0 4YY

CHAPTER ONE

They were robbing the wrong train. Alec Lawson's horse sensed his uneasy mood; the bay snorted and stamped a hind hoof as they waited.

'Easy now, Moray,' he crooned, stroking his horse's shaggy neck. It was early April and here in the Colorado Rockies, horses and men alike had thick winter coats.

Alec flexed his shoulders which ached, after a vigorous session of cutting down lodgepole pines, now laid across the tracks of the railroad, close to where he and the rest of Bill Alcott's gang waited. As the newest member of the group, Alec had done more than his fair share of the work. He'd done so without grumbling; it was important for him to be accepted by the outlaws. If only he'd managed to gain Bill Alcott's trust sufficiently to persuade him to go after the Estes Park to Lucasville express, instead of this one heading for Leadville. Alec's attention was suddenly focused by the puffing of a locomotive approaching along the valley.

Around him, six other men pulled scarves and bandannas over their lower faces, as did Alec. They couldn't quite see the train from their place among the trees that grew not far from the rails, but the sound was getting louder. The horses became more alert, raising their heads and pricking their ears as their riders readied themselves. Alec wasn't afraid, but he felt an undercurrent of unease and distaste about the crime they were about to commit. He wanted it to be over.

The loco gave a blast on its whistle, followed by the hissing of steam as the engineer hurriedly applied the brakes. Cars rattled to a halt as the riders galloped from the trees, their horses kicking up snow. It seemed just a matter of moments before the engineer and fireman were climbing down the cab under the watchful eyes of O'Leary and Manford, while Hannigan covered the brakeman. Bill Alcott, his brother, Jacob, Houston and Alec opened up the express car.

To Alec's relief, the guard made no fuss about opening up the safe. It turned out he'd had little reason to put up a fight. The safe contained a scant five hundred dollars, not the payrolls Alcott had been expecting. While Jacob shouted and swore, Bill Alcott looked around at the other boxes and packages.

'There must be something worth having in some of these,' he said. 'Tie him up,' he said to Houston, indicating the guard. 'You and me'll look through these things. Jacob, you and Turner go see what the passengers have got on them. We'll just have to grab a root with whatever's on this train.'

'Come on then.' Jacob Alcott gestured abruptly to Alec as he turned.

The first car was a Pullman parlour car, as fancy as the lounge of a first class hotel. There was carpet underfoot, tasselled velvet curtains at the windows, and the ceiling was decorated with carved and inlaid panels of polished mahogany. Jacob gave a whistle of appreciation, somewhat muffled by the bandanna over his face.

'This is smart, and then some!' he exclaimed.

There were about half a dozen prosperous businessmen in the car, middle-aged and most sporting various styles of important beards, to make up for the declining hair on the top of their heads. Jacob sauntered up to the first pair, his gun pointed casually at them as they watched fearfully. Alec followed, holding a small burlap bag in one hand and his revolver in the other. He remained tightly focused, flicking glances at the other passengers, and keeping alert for sounds from elsewhere.

'Come on, gents,' Jacob said to the businessmen with great humour. 'Time to make a donation to my favourite charity, that being myself and my pals.'

Alec held out the burlap bag as the two men put in their wallets and watches. One or two of the passengers grumbled as they handed over their things, but mostly they satisfied themselves with angry looks as Alec and Jacob moved along the car. It was the last passenger that Alec felt most uneasy about, and his suspicions proved correct. Jacob let out a low chuckle as he halted by the young woman sitting alone.

'Hey, Turner, we got a real prize here,' he said.

She looked fresh and young, maybe not even twenty yet. Dark chestnut hair was swept up into an elegant style that kept natural curls under control. Wide-set brown eyes and rounded apple-cheeks made her look like the subject of a romantic painting, as though she should have been wearing a medieval dress with trailing sleeves, instead of a fashionable walking suit in bottle green wool.

'Put yer valuables in here, please,' Alec said, holding the bag out to her. He wanted to get this over with as fast as possible.

She retrieved a small, embroidered purse from a pocket hidden in her skirt and dropped that in, then unfastened the jewelled brooch from the lapel of her jacket. She reached towards the bag with it, but Jacob took it from her hand. He held it up so the spring sunlight sparkled on the amethyst and diamond flowers.

'Say, this is a pretty piece, for certain sure, and a swell ring to match an' all.' He held out his hand expectantly.

The young woman glared at him, but pulled the ring off the middle finger of her right hand and thrust it into his palm with a sharp jab. Jacob chuckled, then studied the jewellery thoughtfully, before looking at the girl again. A cunning look spread across his face that worried Alec.

'Fancy jewellery, smart clothes and travelling Pullman class,' Jacob mused. 'You've got kin with plenty of money. I wonder how much they'd give to get you back.' He dropped the jewellery in Alec's bag,

8

then grabbed the girl's arm and started to haul her from the bench seat.

'No!' Alec barked instinctively. Jacob turned to him with a scowl, and with an effort, Alec modified his voice. 'A woman will only slow us down, Jacob. What's she going to ride, anyway?'

'She can ride one of the packhorses,' Jacob said. 'That damn express car hardly had anything worth stealing; we won't need but the one packhorse for that.'

'Look at her,' Alec argued. 'She's a fancy-dressed Easterner. Taking her's a mistake. You got to plan something like a kidnapping.'

'You ain't the bossman of this outfit,' Jacob said scornfully. 'Me and Bill run this gang and if you don't like what we do, you can hand over that bag as soon as we're off this car and light a shuck out of here on your own. Now come on,' he said to the young woman, pulling her arm. 'We've wasted enough damn time already.'

Alec bit down a string of curses and wished more than ever that his boss, the US State Marshal, had asked one of his other deputies to do this job. Bill Alcott and his men had been raiding parts of Colorado for four or five years now, getting bolder and more dangerous as time passed. They hadn't made any raids in Alec's county, which was one of the reasons why Marshal Lindstrom had asked him to undertake this deception, as his face would be less well known to them. Last Fall, Lindstrom and Alec had concocted the identity of Colt Turner, and invented a string of

9

crimes he was supposed to have committed. Reports of Turner's activities had been planted in local newspapers, and rumours spread via talk in saloons. Alec had grown a beard though the winter and spring, letting his dark brown hair get shaggy. It was enough to make him less easily recognisable to anyone who only knew him slightly. He hadn't bothered trying to disguise his natural, Scottish accent though, knowing he could never maintain another for long. He'd also spent time with his new horse, Moray, building up the mutual confidence needed between horse and rider for the best results. His usual mount was a pale dun, and slightly too distinctive for undercover work.

Four weeks ago, Alec had left his senior deputy in charge of county business, and ridden out to find and join Alcott's gang. He'd tried to get them to raid another train, one that would have lawmen waiting aboard, but Bill Alcott hadn't been willing to listen to the newcomer yet.

Jacob Alcott pulled the young woman's arm until she slid out into the aisle, her skirts awry. As he began urging her to the end of the car, she found her voice and exclaimed, 'Oh, please. I need my things.'

'We ain't taking no trunk,' Jacob said, hauling her along.

With a quick look at the cowed businessmen at the other end of the car, Alec holstered his revolver and snatched up the carpet bag from by her seat.

Lacey was manhandled down the steps from the car to the ground by Jacob. He too holstered his gun and pinned her against his side with his arm around her as he bustled her towards the group of men and horses by the express car.

'Look what I found!' Jacob called as they got closer.

Eli Hannigan trotted up, laughing as he inspected Lacey in a way that made Alec's skin crawl. 'Say, that's a fancy piece of baggage you got there.' The swarthily handsome man laughed as the young woman sucked in a sharp breath in indignation. 'Do we all get to share?' he went on, reaching to touch her face.

She swatted his hand away, provoking a rude laugh.

'She's got spunk!' Hannigan exclaimed. 'I like it when they struggle.'

The young woman gulped in a deep breath to hide a sob of fear.

Alec spoke calmly, hoping to reassure her. 'She's no' for messing about with, Eli. Her people will pay well to have her back untouched.'

'They won't know if we've enjoyed her until after we get the money and give her back,' Hannigan pointed out.

Alec stepped around the woman to face him. They were much the same height, but Hannigan was broad-shouldered and more powerfully made than Alec, who dropped the carpetbag as he advanced. Alec didn't hesitate, but glared furiously at the other man.

'This is a decent woman, an' no one lays a finger on her,' he growled. He paused, controlling himself. 'I guess you don't care about breaking your word to anyone, but I promise you, if ye insult this woman, lawmen will be hunting you – all of us – to hell and high water.' His accent had got more pronounced with

11

his anger, the r's exaggerated.

'Hey, break it up!' Bill Alcott spoke as he approached. 'What the hell's going on here, Jacob?'

Jacob laughed. 'I done found us something worth taking on this train after all. This gal's got folks back east that'll pay a fancy price to get her back again. You should see the purty stones she was wearing, Bill.'

Bill tilted his head to one side as he studied the young woman. He was a rangy man with the same pale blue, hooded eyes as Jacob. 'You got family that'll pay five thousand dollars to get you back?' he asked suddenly.

She took a deep breath as she tried to work out what to say. Alec make a quick decision, and spoke up before she replied.

'The brooch and ring she was wearing are worth a few hundred at least. I'd say they've got money enough. They'll pay to get her back safe an' sound.'

She turned to look at him with a hurt expression. Alec looked straight back at her, letting his concern show for a moment before facing Bill again.

'Well, woman, ain't you got a tongue?' Bill demanded.

She straightened her shoulders and lifted her chin as she stared at the outlaw. 'I do, and I have a name. It's Lacey Fry, Miss Fry to you. And yes, my family will pay well to have me given back *unhurt*.'

Jacob laughed. 'You were right, Eli. She's sure got sand to burn. Come on, Bill, with the money for Miss Fry here, we won't need to do another job all summer.'

Bill abruptly made up his mind. 'All right, bring her along. But no squawking or fussin', Missy,' he warned.

'Or there'll be no food and no blankets for you.'

'Come on,' Jacob said to Lacey, and began walking her to the horses.

There were six men in the outlaw gang besides Alec. Lacey did her best to avoid catching their eyes, or hearing the comments passed about her, as she was led to the two pack horses. One horse already carried some blankets and a pair of half-filled packs, the other merely had a hard leather pad with metal rings and straps attached.

'Up you get,' said Jacob, shifting his grip on her.

'She canna ride a pack saddle,' Alec objected, having kept behind them. 'It'll give her sores, an' she'll fall off and slow us up if we go out of a walk. You don't just throw a five thousand dollar statue in the back of a buckboard; it'll get broken.'

Jacob snorted and thrust Lacey at Alec, who had to drop her carpetbag in order to catch her. 'Give me the valuables,' he demanded, holding out his hand for the bag with the stolen goods in it. 'Iffen you care so much about her comfort, she kin ride your hoss, and you can ride the packhorse.' He took the bag and stormed off.

The outlaws were getting ready to leave. O'Leary and Houston had already mounted and were watching the train, guns in hand in case anyone tried to fight back. Alec pulled the neckerchief from his face and looked at Lacey.

'Just stand here quietly,' he said softly. 'I'll do my best for you.'

She looked back at him, eyes wide, making Alec self-conscious of his appearance.

He thought himself to be ordinary looking, though he was actually rather handsome, with large brown eyes and fine regular features that were saved from boyishness by straight, strong brows and a high, arched nose. Lacey broke off her stare, her cheeks flushing. Alec turned to business rather abruptly.

He strapped her carpetbag to the back of the pack-saddle, then turned to her and looked at her thoughtfully.

'I'm sorry, Miss Fry, you'll have to get rid of your bustle. We've got to do a lot of riding, and all those wires will make you pretty uncomfortable.' He paused, and added more hesitantly. 'Can you remove your . . . hoops, wires . . . without taking your skirt off?'

She quickly hid a smile, amused at his discomfort at having to mention unmentionables, and turned away.

'Yes, I think so,' she replied, facing his horse.

Alec turned away from her, watching the other men as Lacey bent to pick up the hem of her skirt and petticoats. There was a lot of rustling, and a mutter that sounded like an objection to corsets. More rustling and a sound of satisfaction followed. A few moments later, she said.

'I'm done.'

Alec turned and an assembly of wires and tapes lay on the ground in front of her, and the back of her dress hung oddly, trailing behind her. He picked the hoops up, moving to throw the bustle towards the railroad tracks. 'We don't want the horses catching their legs in it,' he explained. He studied her again. 'I don't reckon your skirt's full enough to cover your legs when you're sitting cross-saddle. It'll ride up some, mebbe to your knees. If I slit your skirt front and back, it'll hang down, and you can wrap it around your lower legs to keep your modesty and stop the saddle fenders from rubbing.'

Lacey looked as though she wanted to protest: the walking suit of jacket and skirt was clearly new. However, she could see the sense of Alec's suggestion.

'Go ahead,' she said, rather faintly.

With a soft apology, Alec drew the knife from his belt and carefully cut the woollen skirt front and back, from a little below her hip level, to the hem. With that done, he adjusted the stirrups of the saddle for her, then held out his hands to leg her up into the saddle. As she adjusted her petticoats beneath her skirt, the bay horse shifted its weight slightly. Lacey grabbed for the pommel of the saddle.

'Are you all right?' Alec asked.

'Yes, thank you.' Lacey relaxed a little. 'It feels strange, not having the horns of my sidesaddle keeping me secure. And sitting astride feels . . . rather vulgar.' She looked faintly shocked at her own words.

Alec chose to ignore the last part. 'Moray's got smooth paces,' he assured her, patting the bay's neck. 'Just hold onto the pommel if you need to.'

There was a shout from Bill. 'Hurry up, dammit! We need to go.'

As Alec turned to the packhorse, Lacey had a sudden thought.

'There's a shawl in my carpetbag. You can use that to pad the pack saddle.'

15

'Thank you.' Alec quickly opened the bag, took out her fine, woollen shawl, and refolded it into a neat square. Putting it on the pack saddle, he vaulted easily aboard the pack horse. Kneeing it into motion, he took one of the reins of Lacey's mount, and led her away from the train, with the band of outlaws.

CHAPTER TWO

The group was soon moving at a steady jog. The bandits crossed the river, the horses splashing icy cold water as they picked their way across, and headed up one of the steep-sided gulches that entered the main valley where the railroad ran. The April sunshine was warm, but snow glittered on the peaks that surrounded them, and towered overhead.

Alec kept an eye on Lacey, who unashamedly held on to the horn of her saddle as they splashed through the river and when going over rough ground. The deep seat of her saddle, with the high pommel horn and cantle, held her securely, and he could see her beginning to relax as she got used to the feel of riding cross-saddle. Even with the shawl as padding, his own seat was far less comfortable, and he had no stirrups. However, Alec had ridden for many hours in the lightweight McClellen saddle used by the cavalry, so he set himself to simply endure his discomfort while it lasted.

As they moved further up the valley, some of the gang members changed position to ride alongside

Lacey and talk to her. She simply ignored them, refusing to even look at them as they spoke. Manford and Houston quickly got bored at the lack of response and moved away. Hannigan was more persistent, cajoling her at first, and calling her name. When she continued to stare stonily at her horse's ears, Hannigan began a new tack. He started talking about what he'd do to her if her family didn't pay out for her. His descriptions began to get more detailed and lewd, his enjoyment of the situation increasing as Lacey's face flushed red. She shook her head as if trying to shake his filthy words from her ears. Alec could stand it no longer.

'Hauld yer wisht!' he barked, lapsing into his thickest Scottish. 'Have ye no respect? Keep your filth to yourself!'

Hannigan laughed at him. 'Am I embarrassing you, Turner?'

As Alec started to snap back an answer, Bill Alcott halted his horse, bringing the group to a stop, and interrupted.

'Hannigan, shut your mouth. We don't all want to share the depths of your imagination. Save it for the whores you throw your money at. Turner's right, Miss Fry there's a decent woman and you're all to treat her like one. No man's gonna speak foul to her, or lay a finger on her unless I say so. Either no one gets her, or we all do, so there ain't no point in fighting about it. Now, we got a lot of ground to cover, so let's get moving.'

Hannigan spat on the ground between his horse and Lacey's. He cast a sneering look across at Alec before firing his last retort. 'Ain't no use you playing all chivalrous to her; you're scum to her, the same as the rest of us.' He turned his horse and nudged it into a faster jog to get away from them.

Alec bit his tongue and managed not to let fly with the insults he wanted to hurl. He simply couldn't risk provoking the other man too much at the moment. Lacey turned to him, and he saw there were tears in the corners of her eyes.

'Thank you,' she said softly.

Alec merely nodded, too angry still to speak in a civilized tone. He turned his gaze to the beautiful country around them, and waited for the blue skies and fresh smells of the pine forests to work its usual magic on him.

The rest of the bandits talked intermittently amongst themselves as they rode. There was the occasional bout of laughter, at some joke told, and Houston occasionally sang something in a good, bass voice. Alec and Lacey spoke very little, and most of it was to do with their ride. They climbed out of the head of the gulch and turned northwards, entering one of the grassy plateaux that were known in Colorado as parks. Alec studied the surrounding peaks and valleys carefully, trying to get a sense of how this area fitted with the valley where they had ambushed the train. He didn't know this part of the state very well, though he knew roughly where the railroad lines ran, and where the major towns were in relation to them. Studying a printed map was an entirely different matter to finding the way on the ground, especially in the mountains, but he had a good sense of direction, and was building a mental map as they rode.

Alec was also thinking through his situation as they travelled. He couldn't let Miss Fry stay in the hands of these men for any longer than absolutely necessary, even if he was with her. He simply didn't trust them, and he couldn't keep watch over Miss Fry for twenty-four hours every single day. Bill Alcott had ordered her to be left alone, but it was obvious that he wasn't that dedicated to the whole idea of the kidnapping. If there were any difficulties – if they couldn't get a sufficiently prompt reply from her family perhaps – then Alcott might easily decide to give up with the plan and just let his men have her. There was no way Alec would be able to protect her from the rest of the group by himself.

So the only choice he could see was to reveal his identity to her, and to escape with her during the night. He would leave behind his share of the loot from the train, and hope that the bandits would be satisfied with that. Some, no doubt, would want to pursue them though. He'd make for Leadville, where the local law should be good enough to protect them, and wire both the state marshal, Lindstom, and his own deputies in Lucasville. A lot depended on how well Miss Fry could ride. It was time to start talking.

'How are you feeling, Miss Fry? In the saddle, I mean.'

She looked around at his quiet enquiry and Alec saw her hesitate and think, before deciding to answer.

'It's not too bad, thank you. Riding cross-saddle seems to use different muscles to riding aside, and I think I'm going to ache in the morning. But at least I'm not getting sore yet. I hope that pack saddle isn't too bad?'

Alec smiled. 'It's not as good as a proper saddle, but it's a sight more comfortable than sitting bareback on a horse with boney withers.'

Lacey smiled slightly in return. 'I never did ride bareback, of course, but I can guess what it feels like.'

'Have you done much riding back east?' Alec asked.

She nodded. 'Yes, often. I love fox-hunting, especially. It's so thrilling, trying to follow hounds wherever they go. We scramble through some pretty awkward places during a run. It's nothing like this, of course,' she added, gesturing at the mountains.

'The west is a fine place to go riding,' Alec said. 'And I've seen some ladies riding cross-saddle in divided skirts.'

Lacey looked pleasantly shocked at the idea. 'Oh, I wonder if Uncle will let me ride cross-saddle. . . .' The words dried up as she remembered her situation. She looked away again, and Alec thought he heard a faint sniff, as though tears were being held back.

'Keep up your courage,' he said quietly, and let the silence settle back.

Everyone was tired and hungry when they stopped to make camp that evening. Alcott noticed Turner continuing to look after the girl. He helped her down from her saddle, holding on to her as her stiff legs buckled on reaching the ground. She groaned with pain, and clung to him until she recovered her

21

balance. Hannigan jeered at them from beside his own horse.

'Hey, Bill said no one was to touch the lady!'

Turner didn't respond to the taunt, though Alcott saw the girl flinch slightly.

'You can sit here,' Turner said, leading her to a patch of clean grass a short distance from the trees that edged one side of the campsite. 'Wait here an' I'll fetch you your shawl to sit on.'

O'Leary spoke up. 'You just going to leave her standing there, Turner? You should hobble her, like the horses.' The fair-haired, wispy looking man laughed at his own suggestion.

'There's no need,' Turner replied calmly. 'You can see she can barely walk. She canna outrun any of us, she canna mount a horse on her own and she canna carry more than a blanket at most. She's more likely to get hurt or killed trying to run away by herself than if she stays with us.'

'He's right.' Alcott decided to back Turner. 'She'd be as dead as beef in no time iffen she tries to make off on her own.' He stared at the young woman as he spoke and saw the resignation on her face as she accepted the truth. Alcott was pleased; he didn't want the bother of trying to confine her, or guard her. Convincing her not to even try escaping in the first place was much simpler. As he unsaddled his horse and laid out his bedroll, Alcott surreptitiously watched Turner and the girl.

Having settled the girl on her shawl, Turner went to see to the packhorses. Alcott had given him the duty, as the newest member of the group and was pleased by his decision, as Turner had turned out to be knowledgeable and dedicated to the welfare of the animals. Turner brought over the packs with the loot from the robbery and Alcott sorted through it while Turner arranged the rest of the harness to his own satisfaction, and the camp was set up.

Once Turner was done with the horses, he laid out his bedroll close to where the girl was sitting and picking at the dish of beans and rice she'd been given. He spread the saddleblanket beside it, and put one of the blankets from his roll on top of that.

'You can use ma bedroll,' he told the girl, sitting cross-legged beside her. 'It's not fresh an' clean, I know, but it'll be warm enough.'

'Oh thank you,' she answered, as Hannigan sniggered. Lacey looked around at the bedroll and the two blankets beside it. 'Is that all you've got?'

It was going dark now, and a chill was setting in.

'Och, I'll manage,' Turner replied.

'You'd be nice an' cosy iffen you two shared that bedroll,' Hannigan said, making a suggestive gesture with his hands.

'Eli, give Turner one of your blankets,' Bill Alcott ordered.

Hannigan swore, while O'Leary cackled with laughter. 'Why the hell, boss? He's the one fool enough to offer his bedroll to her.'

'Because I warned you about behaving respectful, and I don't want anyone freezing to death in the night,' Alcott answered sharply. 'If Turner ain't around to tend to the packhorses, it'll be your job.'

O'Leary burst into more cackles of high-pitched laughter, which continued into gasps as Hannigan pulled a blanket from his roll and threw it across to Alec, the wind of its passage almost blowing out the small campfire.

'Thank you,' Turner said, aiming his nod of appreciation to Alcott.

Alcott finished up his own plate of hash and lit a cigarette as he mused about the situation. Hannigan was loyal enough, but his crude humour got mighty tiresome after a while. It could be ignored when aimed at gaudily-dressed saloon girls, but didn't seem right when speaking about a decent woman, as Lacey Fry clearly was. Alcott found himself suddenly grateful for Turner's quietly assertive presence. He rather wished he hadn't given in to his brother's idea of kidnapping the woman; Jacob's impulsive ideas could be more trouble than they were worth. In the morning, he'd decide where they were going to take the woman while they waited for her family to pay up, and how to arrange it all. He could talk it over with Chuck, and maybe Turner too. The Scotsman seemed smarter than most of the outlaws Bill Alcott had known. He had an air of quiet confidence, he didn't brag about his doings and he did chores efficiently. Alcott wondered why Turner had turned criminal; he certainly wasn't some feckless ne'er-do-well like O'Leary, or fundamentally lazy, like Hannigan. Alcott suspected Turner would be good at pretty much anything he turned his hand to. If he was reliable, a smart man like

Turner would be a good partner for more ambitious things. Taking him on might have been a stroke of luck after all.

Soon after finishing her food, Lacey silently took herself off to the relative privacy of Turner's bedroll. She only removed her boots and then her jacket, rolling it up for a pillow, before wriggling herself inside the quilts and tarpaulin cover. The men lingered around the dying fire for a little longer. Jacob made a last check on the horses, picketed close by the camp. Pots and dishes were wiped and left ready for the morning. Bill Alcott, Manny Houston, Chuck Manford and Turner played some low-stakes poker as the fire began to die away and Jacob blew a couple of tunes on his mouth organ. After a few hands, everyone was ready to turn in for the night.

Alec woke, shivering and curled into a ball. He took a deep, chilly breath, and stretched out, wriggling his toes and fingers. He rolled onto his back and looked for the moon. From its position, he guessed it to be sometime after midnight, and smiled to himself. He'd wanted to get some sleep, and had been relying on the cold to wake him during the night. His inadequate blankets had certainly made that happen. He let his eyes adjust to the faint light, then rolled again to face Lacey. Alec caught the faint gleam of her eyes looking at him before she closed them, pretending to be sleep.

Fumbling slightly with cold fingers, Alec dug a pocket-knife from the small bag he'd tucked into his roll of blankets. He carefully cut the stitches that had held closed a small pocket added to the inside front of his grey vest, hidden inside the cotton lining. Taking out the small item that had been hidden there for weeks, Alec slithered out of his blankets and held it out to Lacey.

'Take this,' he whispered. 'If you trust me at all, listen to me and take this.'

Her eyes opened and regarded him steadily. Alec found himself holding his breath, and slowly, her arm emerged from the bedroll and took the metal star he was holding out to her. He watched as she felt it, then brought it close to her face and examined it. It was a six-pointed metal star, with a ball tipping each point. The engraving on the centre, barely visible in the moonlight, read *Deputy US Marshal*.

'Ma name's not Turner,' he whispered. 'It's Alec Lawson. I'm a deputy US marshal, and sheriff of Dereham County,' he added with a touch of pride. 'The Alcott brothers and their gang have pulled off some pretty rich robberies in the last couple of years, and killed some folk along the way. Marshal Lindstrom wants them brought in.' He paused, studying Lacey's face. She was looking at him warily, but he felt that she wanted to believe him. 'We've been planning this since last fall. Turner doesn't exist; we made him up so I could pretend to be him. We thought the Alcotts were wintering up near Steamboat Springs so come February, I set out as Turner, hit the outlaw haunts up that way and got myself introduced to them.'

It had been a daunting, nerve-wracking experience, posing as an outlaw and working without the company and backup of his loyal deputies, but Alec didn't have the time to go into the details now.

'I was supposed to get them to rob a specific train, and ma deputies would be waiting for them, but I failed,' he said, frowning slightly. 'Jacob Alcott heard a rumour about a payroll on the train you were on and insisted we went for that. I was hoping it would fail, and I could get them to go for the one we planned. I'm sorry you ended up in this mess,' he finished.

There was a short silence before she spoke. 'It would have been worse if you hadn't been along. They'd have attacked that train anyway, and taken me anyway. And you wouldn't have been there to stop them . . . hurting . . . me.'

Alec let out a silent sigh of relief: she believed him. The relief was immediately followed by a spurt of adrenaline.

'We're leaving now,' he whispered. 'We can get away and make for Leadville. I know you're sore, but I don't know this part of the state too well, and the longer we stay with them, the harder it will be to find ma way to somewhere safe.'

Lacey nodded, and held Alec's badge out to him. He took it with a smile.

'Lie quiet now while I get two horses ready.'

A quick look around, and a chorus of snores, reassured Alec that no one else was awake. After strapping on his gunbelt, he quickly rolled up his blankets and carefully skirted around the sleepers to reach the picketed horses, picking up his saddle and bridle on the way. His bay greeted him with a low nicker as he approached. The others were all used to him and took no notice of his presence among them. Alec had picketed his horse on the far side of the bunch, so it couldn't be easily seen from the fire. With the rest of the horses as a screen, he quietly tacked up his mount, then drifted back through the group, reassuring them with quiet sounds and light touches.

Alec paused in the shadows by the last horse and looked out; everything seemed quiet. He began to step softly forwards, then stopped dead as he heard a grunt and a rustling from the trees. He knew at once that there was too much noise for it to be a wild animal. Alec acted immediately, darting towards the nearest trees, but whoever it was must have been barely out of sight within them. A man appeared in time to glimpse Alec's quick movement, and automatically turned to see what was moving. They were just a few feet apart, close enough to identify one another in the moonlight. Alec saw Jacob Alcott recognise him, see his gunbelt and take a deep breath in order to challenge him. He did the only thing possible: he attacked.

CHAPTER THREE

Jacob hesitated a moment, taken by surprise, then instinctively stepped back half a pace, raising his hands. Alec reached him before he could gather his wits, and punched him hard in the stomach. A half-formed curse burst out as a gasp. Before Jacob could gather breath again to cry out, Alec grabbed the loose neckerchief he wore and pulled it tight around the man's neck. He twisted Jacob hard, getting him off balance so he fell facedown. Alec contrived to fall with him, still grasping the neckerchief, and landed with his knees driving into Jacob's back.

There was a harsh choking sound, swiftly cut off as Alec twisted the neckerchief still tighter, his knuckles digging into the side of Jacob's neck. The outlaw's chest heaved, as he struggled to draw breath. One arm was pinned beneath himself, but the other flailed vaguely. Alec hung on grimly, using his weight to pin Jacob down as he looked towards the camp, searching for any movement among the sleepers. Every sound of the desperate struggle seemed loud to him in the night. As he watched for fresh danger, Jacob abruptly went limp beneath him.

Alec glanced down at the man beneath, not yet daring to loosen his grip. Surely he hadn't been strangling Jacob long enough to kill him? He might only have fainted, and would recover quickly, or be shamming? Alec leaned carefully forward, twisting Jacob's head until he saw the open, unmoving eye. He touched the surface of the eye with the tip of a finger: there was no reaction, no blink. There was no warm breath on a finger held under Jacob's nose. Releasing the neckerchief, Alec stood up, checking on the camp once again. He hadn't intended to kill Jacob, only to silence him so they could make their escape. Alec felt no real remorse, however. Jacob was almost certainly responsible for the deaths of two railwaymen during past robberies. If Alec had been caught trying to flee with Lacey, he would have paid with his life, and she would have no one to protect her. Not that they were clear yet. Alec bent, seized Jacob under his arms, and dragged him a little way into the trees.

There was still no movement in the camp as he re-emerged into the open. Moving as quickly as he could while staying quiet, Alec fetched another saddle and bridle, and tacked up the horse he'd chosen for Lacey. After some thought during the day, he'd picked Manny Houston's dun: it was a sound, well-made trail horse, and got on with his own horse, which was important when travelling in company. It had the good temperament that seemed typical of duns, and Alec thought Lacey would be capable of managing it.

Horses ready, Alec circled back around the camp to where Lacey waited. She slid out of the unfastened tarp, having already donned her boots and jacket.

'What happened?' she whispered as she rose.

'It was Jacob Alcott,' Alec replied succinctly. 'I took care of him.' He gestured to the far end of the roll. 'Help me carry this to the horses; I'll roll it up when we're further away.'

Lacey nodded once. Together they lifted the tarpaulin wrapped bedroll, and carried it around the circle of sleepers to the horses. O'Leary snorted and turned over in his roll as they passed. Lacey stifled a short gasp and froze for a moment, but recovered swiftly, moving along with Alec. He gave her a brief smile of encouragement, concealing his own jumpiness at the movement. Once safely on the far side of the horses, Alec quickly rolled up his bedroll and lashed it into place behind his saddle. Now he paused, looking back towards the campsite.

With Jacob Alcott dead, there was a free bedroll available. Getting it would be risky: it was close to Bill Alcott, and fetching it would take a few more precious minutes, when someone else might wake up. Alec's instincts were urging him to flee, to get away now while he had the chance. But they would only have the one bedroll, plus the blankets and saddle blanket he'd used earlier. It was only April, the nights were still bitterly cold and camping without a proper bedroll, even for just a couple of nights, would be miserable at best and quite possibly fatal.

'We have to get Jacob's bedroll,' Alec told Lacey. He

looked straight at her. 'If we get caught, an' I'm killed, don't try to escape on your own. It'll no' be pleasant with Alcott's gang, but you can't survive out here alone. You'll die for certain.'

Lacey shivered slightly, though Alec couldn't tell if it was from fear or the cold. She moved up beside him, and they moved carefully back to the camp.

With gestures, Alec indicated which end for her to take. Moving slowly, gauging each step carefully, he slipped between the bedrolls to reach the far end of Jacob's empty one. Bill Alcott slept just three feet away; Hannigan was four feet away on the other side. Snores, half-muffled by their bedrolls, were clear enough in the cold air. Keeping his eyes on Lacey's face, Alec crouched and took hold of his end. She copied his movements, rising as he did. The rustling of the tarp-covered roll seemed immensely loud in the night. Alec realized he was holding his breath, and let it out slowly. As he nodded to Lacey and began to step forward, Hannigan let out a grunting snort. Lacey froze, her face screwed up in fear.

Alec halted dead. He could hear her ragged breathing; the bedroll rustled faintly as she shook. A cold sense of fear settled in his stomach: if she panicked now, their chances of escape were slim. Tightly controlling his own nerves, Alec acted calm. He tugged gently on the bedroll to gain her attention. Her eyes widened and she looked at him, her mouth slightly open as though on the point of screaming.

'It's all right,' Alec said, his voice as low and as soft as if addressing a frightened horse. 'Breathe, lassie, breathe slow and gentle.'

She stared back at him, as though unsure what he'd said. Alec took a slow, deep breath himself and let it out gently. After a moment, Lacey did the same. Alec smiled as she continued, and the terror began to ease from her face.

'Calm and quiet,' he whispered. 'Let's move.'

Lacey swallowed, then nodded.

'Now,' said Alec, and together they carried the bedroll away from the campfire and back to the horses.

Jacob Alcott's overcoat had been tucked inside the bedroll as a pillow; Alec pulled it out and passed it to Lacey. She arranged her shawl over her head and shoulders before pulling the coat on over her jacket. His woollen gloves were in the pockets, so she put them on over her own thin, leather ones. The bedroll was swiftly rolled and lashed behind Lacey's saddle. Alec boosted her up, then quickly and quietly moved amongst the horses, soothing them with a pat and quiet sounds as he unfastened the picket ropes from their halters. He didn't expect them to wander far, but they might drift away from the camp, or at least play hard to catch in the morning when the outlaws wanted them. He didn't try to scare them or lead them away in a group, for fear of the noise they might make. With that last job done, Alec swung neatly into his own saddle, settling happily into the comfortable seat, and smiled at Lacey. She smiled back, though with anxious eyes. Nudging his horse into a walk, Alec led them away from the outlaws' camp.

*

Alec didn't bother seeking cover as they rode in the dark. He stayed out on the open grassland where the light was better. Lacey was looking around, letting her horse choose his own path. She didn't dare speak until they were half a mile from the camp, and even then she spoke softly.

'It's so beautiful. And so clear!'

Snow on the upper slopes and the peaks glittered silver in the moonlight. Above was a wide sweep of sparkling stars scattered across the sky, so many more than were visible in a city. The whole world around them was outlined in frost. As they topped a low rise, they startled some elk, which bounded away in great leaps. Both horses and riders had warmed up some, and Alec felt it was time to increase the pace. He urged them into a steady jog. Lacey made some small complaining noises at first, still stiff after the previous day's riding. She bore the discomfort bravely though and gradually seemed to settle.

She rode more or less alongside Alec, who kept an eye on her. After nearly half an hour, he could see that she was getting looser in the saddle, clinging to the pommel more and hauling herself straight in the seat more frequently. She still didn't complain, but he could hear soft hisses of discomfort. He slowed to a walk again, praising her for her endurance.

'It's helping me keep warm,' Lacey answered, somewhat breathlessly.

'Take your feet out of your stirrups an' stretch your

legs,' he advised.

She did so, half-smiling. 'That's not something you can do when riding aside.'

'I guess not,' Alec replied.

They continued to walk and jog at intervals, pacing themselves as they rode through the night.

It was while they were walking that Alec's horse slowed, lowering its head to inspect the ground more closely.

'Slow,' he ordered quickly, holding out his arm.

Lacey hardly needed to slow her mount, which was also walking more cautiously.

'What is it?' she queried. The ground ahead looked much the same as that they'd just passed through.

'Moray knows something,' Alec replied, nudging his horse to walk on a little. 'These are good trail horses; it's wise to listen to what your horse tells you.'

As he spoke, he could hear his horses hoofs squelching in soft ground. Moray took another step, and lurched slightly as his front hoof sank to the fetlock. The horse jerked himself back with a snort, Alec sitting easily in the saddle.

'The ground's boggy here. We hafta go round this low patch.'

Lacey followed as Alec turned his horse, letting it pick its way around the edge of the soft ground. He patted his horse's neck, grateful to it for not blundering into the bog. They were headed away from the river, towards the peaks that bordered the grassy park. He was both mentally and physically tired, and it had to be worse for Lacey. Travelling at night was dangerous at the best of times; as much as he wanted to get as far away from the outlaws as possible, they needed to find somewhere to hide and rest. As they headed further away from the river, Alec picked out a side valley leading up into the peaks, and headed for it.

'We'll make camp in that valley,' he told Lacey, reassuring her that the cold, tiring ride had an end.

It took the best part of an hour, but at last they were settled in a wooded clearing. Sitting on his bedroll, Alec eased off his boots with a quiet sigh, wriggling his toes. He relished the chilly air on his feet for a few moments, before sliding his legs inside the quilts, keeping his socks on. The boots were placed handily close by, with his hat atop them to keep them dry, then Alec finally snuggled down inside his bedroll, fastening the tarp. He glanced once at Lacey, a few feet away inside her own bedroll, and then at the tethered horses, grazing the frosty grass nearby. Alec stretched out, then relaxed, and finally fell deeply and properly asleep.

It was a couple of hours past dawn when he woke again. After the first drowsy moments, Alec came fully awake fast, lifting his head out of the bedroll to look around. The camp was quiet, but his movement prompted a soft whinney from his horse, which watched him with ears pricked, hoping for food. Alec smiled and relaxed. The sound woke Lacey too. She moved, and groaned in pain, mumbling something before erupting into a sitting position, her wavy hair hanging in untidy loops. She gazed around with a look of dismay on her face, finally settling on Alec.

'Oh, gosh. Oh gosh, oh gosh, oh gosh, oh Hell!' She covered her face with her hands. 'I was hoping it was a dream,' she moaned, and began sobbing.

Alec's heart sank; he'd been so pleased and relieved at how well Lacey had coped with the situation the day before, that he'd begun to assume that she'd continue in the same way. He had no idea how to cope with a sobbing woman. Should he leave her to cry it out, or try to comfort her – and if so, how? For a few moments he had the urge to simply pull his quilts back over his head and hope for the problems to go away: crying women, outlaws, consciousness, even. Alec sighed. Tempting though the idea was, it wouldn't solve anything. He had to do something, and the first thing to do was get out of his cosy bedroll.

Alec set about the morning tasks of camp as though everything was normal. He refreshed himself, took the horses to a nearby creek to drink, then fed them both some of the grain he'd taken from the outlaws' supplies. By the time he'd done this, Lacey had stopped crying. She was sitting up in her bedroll, wearing Alcott's coat, and brushing out her hair. Alec returned to the bedrolls and opened a saddle-bag.

'It'll have to be a cold breakfast, I'm afraid,' he said. 'I dare not light a fire; the smoke would give us away.'

'All right,' Lacey replied in a small voice.

Alec took out a lump of cheese and some crackers. 'How are you feeling this morning; are you sore?'

'I ache,' she said decidedly. 'And my legs are sore where the saddle rubbed.'

Alec thought for a moment. 'I have a spare pair of trousers you could borrow,' he suggested hesitantly.

'Trousers? Oh, no, I couldn't!' Lacey exclaimed. She paused, pursing her mouth as she thought. 'I'd rather not if I could help it. I mean, I could sew up my skirt to make a proper divided skirt, but I don't have needle and thread,' she finished unhappily.

Alec opened another saddle-bag. 'I do, you can borrow my housewife.' He took out a small fabric bundle and tossed it across to her.

'Thank you.' Lacey unrolled the bundle to reveal needles, thimble, flat skeins of thread, three safety pins and a pair of small scissors all tucked into pockets. She looked at them, then suddenly smiled and looked at Alec. 'A housewife! I should have realized before. My father served in the War, and my mother's family are mostly military. I made a housewife for Cousin Tom. You were in the Army, weren't you?'

'Aye,' Alec admitted proudly. 'I was in the Fifth Cavalry. I served ten years, and made captain.'

Lacey studied him, shaking her head slightly. 'I thought you seemed different to the other outlaws – the real outlaws, I mean. They treated you like a bit of an outsider, but you acted like a man used to giving orders, not taking them.'

'It wasna' easy,' Alec agreed. 'I've gotten used to command. Ma deputy sheriffs all served with me so I'm still commanding the same men.'

A cool breeze gusted across Alec's face, bringing him back from thoughts of his friends back home.

'We need to get moving,' he said briskly. 'I'll get

some breakfast now, while you fix your skirts, then I'll get the horses ready. You can eat when you're done sewing, or in the saddle if necessary.'

Lacey had worked her hair into a long braid, and pinned it up in an untidy coil on the back of her head. She picked up the housewife and gave it a malevolent look.

'I never liked sewing, but at least this isn't a sampler,' she said in tones of infinite scorn. 'Samplers are just so pointless. All they do is hang on the parlour wall and get pointed out to young men who visit, like an advertisement for how good you'll be as a wife. It's demeaning, like being advertised for sale like a horse. For sale, one prospective wife. Well broken and quiet to handle. Has seen hounds,' she added with a giggle.

Alec laughed too, relieved that she'd got her sense of humour back. He turned so he was facing away from her as she wriggled her skirt and petticoat off inside the bedroll, and began eating his cold breakfast.

CHAPTER FOUR

'It's so warm already!' Lacey exclaimed.

Alec looked across at her with a smile as they rode. 'It's like that in the mountains,' he replied. 'Gets so cold at night and warms up quickly in the day. I was told it's because the air's thin up here.'

'How can air be thin?' she asked incredulously.

'I don't understand myself,' Alec replied. 'It just is when you're higher up, an' we're about eleven thousand feet above sea level here, mebbe more. That's why the air is so clear in the mountains,' he said appreciatively. 'With the air being thin, you can feel it when you do harder work. Some folk are more bothered by it than others, but you can get out of breath pretty easily up here.'

'Well, I feel fine now,' Lacey replied.

'Good.'

She looked to be all right too. Alec had no idea how she'd managed her petticoat, but Lacey was sitting quite comfortably in her saddle, with the divided skirt hanging well on either side. The going wasn't too bad here, the horses moving at a steady walk as they warmed up for the day's travel. The gulch that Alec had ventured up during the night curved sharply before opening up into the main park. They were heading back down the gulch, on the sunnier side of the valley to enjoy the warmth.

Thinking about the bandits, Alec did some mental calculations and pulled his horse to a gentle stop. Lacey halted beside him, her expression changing from relaxed to anxious.

'I reckon the sun rose a good couple of hours back,' Alec said. 'Alcott and the others would have woken soon after, and found we were gone, and Jacob was dead. I'm guessing Alcott would come after us as soon as possible, once they'd buried his brother. They couldn't travel too fast – they'd be watching for our trail – but they could be pretty close to the mouth o' that gulch about now.'

'Really?' Lacey sat straighter in her saddle, as if ready to whirl her horse around. 'They might have gone the other way; maybe they thought we'd headed back towards the pass over to the railroad?' she suggested.

'I was kinda hoping that myself,' Alec admitted. 'But I've heard Manford bragging on his skill at following a trail. You wait here, and I'll climb that spur of land to see if I can spot them.'

'All right.'

As he rode forwards, Alec was pleased that Lacey dismounted to rest her horse as she waited. He angled his horse across the side of the spur, zig-zagging back

41

and forth to make the climb easier. Alec let the horse choose his own footing, and Moray picked his way carefully over the ground, where rocks were often concealed in the patches of snow. Alec halted below the crest of the hill, and tied his horse to a scrubby juniper bush. Bending and moving cautiously, Alec approached the top of the spur. He used a cluster of rocks as cover, avoiding the patches of snow that crunched beneath his boots as far as possible. By going carefully, often on hands and knees, Alec found a spot between two rocks where he could lie and look out into the park beyond, almost as far up as the mouth of the gulch.

He heard the bandits before he spotted them. They were gathered about a quarter of a mile from the mouth of the gulch, four of them watching as Manford scouted on foot. Houston was now riding Jacob Alcott's horse, and leading one of the packhorses, while O'Leary had the other. Alec could catch their voices, though not the words. There was a brief bout of wild laughter from O'Leary, before Alcott turned and said something that silenced him. Manford turned and called to them, He gestured towards the gulch, and nodded in reply to something shouted by Alcott. Alec had seen enough. Backing away carefully, as soon as he could, he began trotting back towards his horse.

Back in the saddle, he pushed his horse into a jog, trusting to its surefootedness. Lacey watched his approach for a few moments, then led her horse to a low rock and used it as a mounting block to get herself back in the saddle. She was ready to move as soon as

42

Alec got back to her.

'You saw them?' she asked, turning her horse as he reached her.

Alec nodded. 'Manford found our trail. They don't know where in the gulch we are, so they won't be moving faster than a trot or their horses will tire too quickly in case they have to ride a long way to find us. We've got a wee start on them so let's be making the most of it.' Alec shook his reins, and Moray leaped forward into a brisk lope; Lacey followed him half a length behind.

He kept the pace up for almost half an hour, when the gulch had curved again. Alec eased up the pace, aware that he was breathing a little more heavily than he'd expect after such a ride. He studied the horses too as they walked on; both were taking longer than usual for their breathing to slow to the normal rate. Lacey, though, looked fine. Alec felt mildly indignant that she was coping with the thin air better than himself, but was also relieved; it was one less thing to worry about.

The valley stretched away ahead of them, white-clad peaks all around. A narrower gulch led away on their left. Alec considered things as they rode in the bright sunshine. The folds of the land and stands of pine offered some cover along the main valley, but it would be hard to keep moving and keep out of sight. If they took the smaller gulch to the left, they wouldn't be immediately visible to anyone coming around into the main valley. It offered less cover though.

'If the bandits are blocking us from leaving this

valley, what are we going to do?' Lacey asked.

Alec indicated the mountains ahead. 'We crossed them yesterday; there'll be a pass we can take to get back into the Arkansas River valley. With any luck, we can reach Buena Vista tomorrow.'

'Oh, I'm looking forward to sleeping in a proper bed again.'

'We'll go this way,' Alec said, with more confidence than he felt, as he turned towards the smaller gulch. He knew his own county well, but it was northwest of here. This, the Sawatch Range, he only knew in the most general way. He had no idea if there was a pass across at the head of either valley, but he was confident he could find the way if there was one.

As they crossed the floor of the valley, they reached their first obstacle. The creek was full and fast as the snows started to melt. There was no obvious trail across, and Alec rode along the bank a little way, considering the fast flowing water.

'There's no telling how deep it is, or what the bed's like,' he said to Lacey. 'If there's rocks under the water, the horses could fall. It would be easy to drown in fast water like that, or the horse could lame itself.'

'I can't swim,' Lacey replied.

Alec glanced back down the gulch. 'We can't take too long.' He assessed the bank again. 'It's no more than ten feet. A horse covers near on that much in one stride at the gallop. Our horses can clear that easy enough. You jumped obstacles out hunting, didn't you?'

'Sure I did,' Lacey said. 'But I was riding side-saddle;

I had the pommel horns to hold me on.'

'You stayed on because you gripped the pommel horns with your legs. You've got a cantle and pommel on that saddle to hold you, and you can grip the horse's sides with your legs and take a hold of his mane with your free hand. Get him going well and give him plenty of rein as you jump. He'll do it fine,' Alec reassured her. 'I'll go first an' he'll want to follow. Just jump the same place I do.'

He looked at Lacey and got a nod from her, then circled Moray away from the bank at a trot. Picking his spot, Alec urged the horse into a controlled gallop, increasing speed until they reached the bank. Moray leapt boldly outward, Alec light and firm in the saddle. The horse landed well clear and came back sweetly to hand. Alec slowed him and circled back to face Lacey, on the other bank, grinning with pure pleasure.

'Your turn,' he called.

Lacey followed his example, riding a circle away from the creek to get her horse going, then increasing speed as she approached the jump. Alec could see she was tense, clutching the reins with one hand and the mane with the other, but not pushing the horse on properly. She didn't keep her mount straight on the course that Alec had followed either.

'Gallop!' he yelled.

Lacey half-panicked, thumping her heels against the horse's side as it placed itself for the jump. It took off slightly too soon, and not fast enough. The dun stretched itself valiantly over the icy water as Lacey lurched in the saddle. Its front legs reached the bank safely but its back legs landed on a snow overhang that crumpled, dropping its quarters down into the creek. Lacey squealed, grabbing for the mane on the crest of its neck with her rein hand. The horse floundered against the edge of the bank as Alec kicked his own horse forward.

'Let go of the mane!' he yelled. 'Let him get his head forward.'

Lacey did as she was told, grabbing the pommel with both hands. The dun got his head down and hauled himself onto the bank of the creek. He trotted forward a few paces and stopped as Alec caught his bridle. Lacey continued to cling to the saddle, gasping, as the dun shook himself, but she pulled herself together enough to pat the horse. Alec dismounted and calmed her horse, talking to it and pulling its ears through his hands. When it was quieter, he examined its legs and hoofs, satisfying himself that no damage had been done. Giving it a final pat on the rump, he looked sternly at Lacey, his dark eyes fierce.

'I told ye to jump where I did. The bank wasna' firm where you jumped,' he barked.

'I'm sorry, Sheriff. I was nervous.' Lacey sniffed, her voice tremulous.

It was being addressed as 'sheriff' jolted Alec into remembering that he was not an officer addressing a new recruit. He now registered Lacey's distress, and anger turned to guilt. He patted the horse again.

'I'm sorry, Miss Fry,' he said more gently. 'I didn't mean to upset ye. But you must do as I tell you; you could have lamed your horse jumping there.'

'I'll try,' Lacey promised.

'Good.' Alec flashed a quick smile, and swung himself into his saddle. 'We'd best be getting on.'

They followed Chuck Manford's lead, though the trail wasn't too hard to follow here. Bill Alcott looked relaxed in the saddle of his liver chestnut, though he tensed slightly every time he saw Manny Houston on Jacob's horse. That was just wrong, and he kept expecting Jacob to start shouting at Houston to get off of his horse and ride his own. But Turner had made off with Jacob's horse and the woman, and had killed Jacob. Alcott felt kind of numb about his brother's death, but also angry. Angry at Turner for betraying him, and angry at himself for his lapse in judgement in letting that little Scots bastard join him. He'd trusted Turner, and even started to like him, and now the two-faced skunk had gone and stolen the woman away, after all his protestations about not taking her, and then on treating her right.

'How'd you reckon Turner got her to sneak away with him?' Houston asked Hannigan. The half-caste had been angry at having his horse stolen, and wasn't happy about riding the dead man's mount. He'd spent the first half hour or so grumbling about his bad luck until Manford had told him to shut up. 'Sure an' they can't have made much noise iffen Jacob was the only one they done woke up.'

Hannigan snorted. 'It was all that gentleman hogwash he pulled, making out he was real respectful of her. I bet my bottom dollar she sure got a surprise once he got her on her lonesome.'

'I guess Turner don't like sharing much,' Houston said.

'He wanted to be certain-sure he got the cherry.' Hannigan spat disdainfully.

Up ahead, Manford had reined in and was studying the ground. The other outlaws stopped too, not wanting to trample any trail. After scouting around a little, he gestured for them to join him.

'See that there?' he pointed out a pile of horse dung a little way up the side of the spur. 'Someone waited there a spell while someone else climbed to the top. Then the climber returned and they both done rode back up the gulch. Pretty damn recent, too.'

'Turner climbed up to scout and saw us coming,' Alcott said, looking at the top of the spur and estimating the view it gave across the park below.

'There's older tracks leading up here,' Manford said. 'Maybe sometime yesterday. And fresh ones coming back, then returning up the gulch.'

'Came up here last night, most likely camped in that patch of wood. Came back this way this morning, saw us, and headed back up to the divide,' Alcott summarized.

'How far ahead d'you reckon they are?' O'Leary asked excitedly, gathering up his reins and making his horse dance restlessly.

'It don't matter,' Alcott said. He smiled for the first time that day as he looked along the gulch. 'Turner ain't so smart after all. He ain't gonna get out over those peaks. There's no pass; he'll have to come back

48

this way with his tail between his legs.'

'So let's go meet him,' O'Leary said, grinning.

'No need to wear out ourselves an' the hosses,' Alcott said. 'Let Turner and the girl ride all day; they'll end up coming back unless they want to die up there. We'll make camp in those trees ahead, where the gulch is narrowest, an' be waiting for them to ride right back to us. They can't stay bottled up in this gulch for long. They'll have to try and leave and we'll be right there, all rested and ready.' He looked along the gulch and smiled once again.

At first, Alec and Lacey kept up a fair pace, jogging for half a mile at a time then slowing to a walk before either horses or riders got too out of breath. The trees became sparser and smaller as they climbed higher and there was more snow. It became too risky to go faster than a walk, and often a slow one at that, as the horses picked their way between rocks and round or through the snow. Alec glanced back at intervals, but he neither heard nor saw anything of the bandits. They did once spot three bighorn sheep trotting away across a rock face, and a golden eagle soared overhead for a while. The sun moved past noon, and the going got harder. They zig-zagged back and forth across the gulch, eyes screwed up against the dazzling brightness of the snow. Both riders had removed coats and jackets and the horses' necks were damp with sweat from the warmth of the sun as well as exertion.

Halting, so they could all catch their breath, Alec

shaded his eyes with his hand and studied the land-scape around them. Whichever way he looked, he was forced to the same conclusion.

'It's no good,' he said, wheezing slightly. 'We canna cross the mountains here.'

'What?' Lacey gasped back. She had one hand pressed against her slender waist. For the first time, Alec realized that of course she must be wearing a corset, making it harder for her to breathe deeply of the thin air.

'I chose wrong,' he said sharply, annoyed with himself. 'There's no pass here. I doubt we can get across here, even afoot. If we try, we'll have to sleep out on the mountains, in the snow tonight, at best.'

'What would be the worst?' Lacey asked.

'We die on the trail or freeze during the night,' Alec said bluntly.

Lacey did nothing other than simply gasp for a few moments. 'We have to go back?' she asked eventually.

Alec nodded. 'Now, so we can get down from here and set up camp before dark.'

'What about the bandits?' Her face tightened.

Alec paused, listening again for the sound of other riders, before he answered. 'I don't think they followed us up here,' he said. 'We'll go cautiously, but I'd rather take my chances with them than with the mountain.'

Lacey gave a resigned nod. 'I'm hungry.'

Alec looked around till he saw a patch some quarter of a mile away, where there was some bare rock and shadow. He pointed towards it. 'We'll eat there,' he promised.

Lacey nodded again, and let him turn and pass her before turning her own horse to follow him back down again.

Once there, Lacey dismounted with a faint groan, and staggered off to sit in the welcome shade. Alec unsaddled both horses, laying the saddle blankets out upside-down in the sun. He watered the horses at a creek, fed them some grain, then rubbed the damp from their necks and backs with a cloth. Spreading that out in the sun too, with stones to hold it down in the wind, he checked the horses' legs and hoofs. Only then did he sit down near Lacey and start on his own helping of cheese and crackers.

'Aren't you going to groom them as well?' she enquired drily.

'Not until the sweat's dried. It'll brush out then,' Alec replied. He caught her surprised expression. 'Would ye like to walk to Leadville, carrying all your own things?' he asked.

Lacey shook her head, looking sheepish. 'I know we need to look after the horses; I just didn't realize there was so much work, grooming them so often.'

'See how the hair under the saddle is hard, and not as smooth as on the flanks,' Alec said, pointing at Moray. 'They canna roll here, so brushing will get the dried sweat from their skin and make them comfortable before the saddles go back. The more comfortable a horse is, the longer and harder it can work for you.'

Lacey nodded. 'That's common sense, really – horse sense,' she added with a laugh.

'Aye,' Alec answered, smiling before he bit into the cheese.

Going down the gulch again was easier, but still needed caution. Their trail showed clearly, with the snow, which worried Alec. He took advantage of what cover there was and halted frequently to listen, or to scout ahead a little way, often on foot. The need for constant alertness at least meant he didn't have time to dwell on his mistake, or the difficulties ahead. After a final, careful check, they emerged back into the main gulch. Alec looked towards the head, at the snowy peaks there, and decided not to risk it. They'd already wasted one day on a dead end; it was better to aim for somewhere he was more sure of finding a pass across the mountains. Instead, he led the way back towards the creek.

'We'll jump it like before,' he said, gathering up his reins and preparing to increase his pace.

'No!' The word burst out of Lacey. 'I can't do it.'

Alec halted and looked at her. 'You jumped it once already. The horses can do it easily, you know that.'

'No, I don't want to. Please don't make me do it,' she begged.

'Why so scared?' Alec asked, forcing himself to speak gently. 'You made a mistake last time but there was no harm done. You'll not do it again.'

Lacey shook her head, fiddling with her reins in a way that made her horse toss its head. 'I still don't feel safe in this saddle; I don't know how to sit to the jump. I know I don't, now. And I ache, I don't feel strong enough to sit tight. I'm not like you; I'm just a woman.'

There was some truth in the babble of excuses. It was clear enough to Alec that she was genuinely worried by the thought of taking the jump, though he felt she was perfectly capable of it. What was important was that her fear would affect the way she approached the jump. and the way the horse itself jumped. All manner of things could lead to disaster and Alec couldn't risk either Lacey or her horse getting hurt.

'All right.' He gave in. 'We'll head back along this side of the creek and try to find somewhere to cross lower down.'

The tension immediately left her body. 'Oh, thank you, Sheriff. Thank you so much.'

'Come on.' Alec nudged his horse into a walk again, following the north bank of the creek.

Alec kept within the edge of the treeline as much as possible, but the lodgepole pines often grew closely crowded together, making it impossible to pass between them. They picked their way along as the gulch curved in the first part of the S-shape it made before entering the main park. The other side of the gulch, the spur that Alec had climbed in the morning, was in deep shadow now. Alec was feeling increasingly uneasy about the location of the bandit group. He'd been sure that they'd found his trail leading up this gulch, and would be following him. Why hadn't they followed this way? Alec thought back to the weeks he'd spent with the outlaws. Riding this way, it had been clear that Alcott knew this area well. It was the clue that Alec needed; he guessed exactly what the outlaw had done. The only question now was exactly where the outlaws would be waiting for them. Alec needed more information.

He halted his horse. 'Wait here an' stay out of sight,' he instructed, dismounting.

He heard Lacey dismounting too as he made his way cautiously to the edge of the trees and looked out along the gulch. Carefully studying the landscape, Alec compared it to what he'd seen from the top of the spur earlier, trying to work out where the bandits might be, and how to continue on without being seen. There was a patch of trees ahead where the gulch curved the other way, and he recalled another one where it opened out into the main park.

There were no tracks he could see in the snow, no indication that the bandits had even come this far up the gulch after them. Alcott was smart; he'd pick the narrowest part of the gulch to lay in wait for his quarry. In which case, he was probably in that nearer patch of trees. Alec studied the ground again, before moving. Using all the cover he could find, he gradually got closer to the cluster of pines, aspens and scrub. A little over one hundred yards away he had to halt, hidden by a shallow hollow in the ground and some scrubby silverberry bushes. Staring at the trees, he tried to pick out shapes within them. Alec couldn't tell if he were imagining movement, or glimpses of colour. Then he suddenly heard O'Leary's wild laugh. The bandits were there, and not too far away either.

CHAPTER FIVE

Moving as cautiously as before, Alec worked his way back to Lacey and told her what he'd discovered.

'We'll go back a ways and make our own camp,' he told her. 'Once it gets dark we can light a fire an' have something hot to eat and drink. We'll rest up, and sneak past them afore dawn.'

'Couldn't we wait until they give up and go away?' Lacey asked. 'We left them the money from the train; surely they won't stay another full day. Won't there be lawmen from Leadville out searching for them now?'

'Mebbe,' Alec replied. 'But I killed Alcott's brother an' for all they know, I stole you away to get the ransom for myself. Bill Alcott won't be giving up so easily.'

Lacey's face went tense and screwed up, as though she were trying hard not to cry. Alec watched help-lessly, until she gave a large sniff and plastered a weak smile on her face.

'I'm sorry,' she said quietly. 'It's just all so horrible.'

'Whisht, lassie, I'll get you back to your family, I

swear,' Alec promised, unable to think of any other way of comforting her.

When Lacey nodded, he mounted and led them back along the gulch, once again retracing their steps.

Alec found them a place to camp that was out of sight of the trees where the bandits were. When he got back from watering the horses, he saw that Lacey had spread the saddle blankets out in a golden patch of evening sun to air, and was gathering firewood.

'I hope this is all right,' she said. 'I only ever used coal or boughten logs before, and never built a fire outside.'

'It's grand of you,' Alec said, with a smile. He gave her some suggestions about what to look for, and tended to the horses.

Not until it was almost fully dark did Alec finally light the fire. Supper was a basic stew of bacon and beans, with hot coffee, but it was filling and welcome. Lacey volunteered to clean the dishes and things in a patch of snow and all but the coffee pot and a couple of tin mugs were soon packed away neatly in the saddle-bags. Alec took out his pocket watch and wound it, checking the time by the flickering firelight.

'We need to move before full daylight,' he told Lacey. 'Could you stay awake until midnight, and then wake me?'

'I think so,' she replied. Rest, and hot food had restored her morale and she looked relaxed as she sat on her bedroll, brushing her chestnut hair. 'I was so excited when Uncle Peter and Aunt Pat invited me to come and visit in Leadville. I thought it would be an adventure.' She snorted. 'I guess I got the adventure, sleeping rough and being chased by outlaws. And with a man I hardly know.' She stopped and gave an embarrassed giggle. 'I'm sorry, you've been a gentleman. But . . . it's shocking really.'

'We dinna have much choice,' Alec replied simply. 'I aim to get you back to your family as soon as I can,' he added sincerely. He handed her the watch. 'Midnight, remember. I'll be waking you soon after five and we'll be on our way again.'

Lacey nodded. 'Midnight,' she promised.

Alec settled himself inside his bedroll. It did indeed feel strange to be travelling with only a young woman, and simple things like nipping behind a tree to urinate suddenly seemed a lot more awkward. The idea of sleeping, and leaving her on guard, to wake him later also seemed wrong, but he couldn't think of another solution. They needed to be moving before dawn, and without an alarm clock, someone had to stay awake. Well, there wasn't anything he could do about it tonight. With years of practice, Alec firmly put aside worries he couldn't deal with at the moment, and relaxed into sleep.

Alec had coffee brewing and a pan of beans and molasses warming over the fire before he woke Lacey in the pre-dawn dark. She grunted resentfully and burrowed further down inside the bedroll.

'You have to get up,' Alec said.

'No.' Her voice was muffled but determined. 'It's

cold out there.'

Alec sighed. He was cold too, but staying in their bedrolls would get them nowhere. 'You can come out into the cold now, and let me get you to safety, or you can lie in there and let Alcott and his men come looking for us. And when they find us, they'll kill me and drag you out of there anyway and you know what they'll do to you.'

There was a muted wail of frustration and despair, then, as Alec wondered if he'd been too blunt, her head popped out of the covers. She glared at him resentfully in the firelight.

'I hate this mess!' Lacey said viciously.

'I'm no' too fond of it myself,' Alec remarked drily.

She hissed like an angry cat, then unsnapped fastenings on her tarp and sat up quickly, shaking out the coat she'd been using as a pillow and slipping it on.

'This is awful,' she grumbled, wrapping her shawl over her head.

Alec moved back to the fire and poured her a mug of coffee. Wriggling out of the bedroll, Lacey came to the fire, reaching for the mug. Huddled in layers of clothing and shivering, she held the cup to her face.

'Thank you,' she muttered, flashing a half-apologetic glance.

As Alec cleaned the dishes after eating, Lacey began the process of putting her hair up, trying to pin the long braid into a coil on the back of her head.

'Oh, this can be such a nuisance,' she muttered, pulling pins out and stabbing them in again. 'I can't do it with gloves on and my fingers are so cold and stiff without.'

Alec hesitated, half-wondering if he should offer to help, but not having the slightest idea how to pin a woman's hair up.

'Oh!' Lacey pulled all the hairpins out altogether, letting the braid fall loose down her back. 'What does it matter if my hair's up?' she said sharply, casting Alec a defiant look. 'I know a lady should, in public, but what does it matter out here? You're the only person who's going to see me, and you've seen me *sleeping*, for heaven's sake!'

Alec thought of his mother, and could only remember seeing her with her hair down on the few occasions he'd seen her in her nightclothes. Dark hair, she'd had, as dark as his own. 'If it's in a plait, it won't get in your face,' he said. 'You don't want it loose with the winds we have in the mountains.'

'Braided is fine,' Lacey said, and dropped the hairpins into her carpetbag with an air of satisfaction.

They were soon on their way again, this time riding along the floor of the gulch, away from the trees. The sky was a deep indigo, lit by crowded stars that threw light onto the layers of snow around them. There was enough light for them to ride with some confidence, trusting to the horses to find their way safely. It was quiet, with the soft steps of the horses and the slight creaking of saddles far louder than in the day. The horses pricked their ears to the wail of a coyote, but neither seemed disturbed by its presence. As they drew close to the trees where the bandits were camping, Alec halted and gestured for Lacey to lean close so he could speak softly to her.

'I'm hoping they're on the other side of the creek, but we must be careful; there may be someone on watch. Follow me, and let your horse pick his trail.'

'All right,' she said, her trust in him clear in her face.

Alec hoped he was doing the right thing, but his choices were severely limited.

He set off again, keeping as close to the side of the gulch as the trees would allow. The rustling of the undergrowth, and crunch of snow seemed horribly loud in the quiet night. It was far darker too, under the trees, and Alec had to rely almost entirely on his horse. More than once, he had to deviate from his path, or even retrace his steps as they wound their way through the tangle of pines. Lacey dropped back a couple of lengths, to let him have more room to manoeuvre. After some five minutes of cautious, slow movement, Alec caught the familiar scent of woodsmoke. He halted, and turned his head, trying to establish the direction of the changeable wind. After a few seconds he was sure the smoke was coming from the other side of the creek. If there was smoke, it meant there must be someone awake. His heartrate jumped another notch, but Alec didn't let any fear show on the outside. As they moved on, the wind changed again and blew towards the camp.

The quiet was broken by a loud neigh from the other side of the creek; one horse calling to another.

Before Alec could do more than swear under his breath, Lacey's horse called back to its old companions. There was more neighing and rustling, as the unseen horses responded to the presence of friends, almost drowning Hannigan's voice as he shouted for the others to wake up. Alec pressed his legs to his horse's sides, urging it on. He wanted to flee, every instinct telling him to get away as fast as possible, but he had to hold to a brisk walk while in the dark trees.

Alec glanced back over his shoulder and saw that Lacey was following, in control of her horse though its head was turned towards the creek. Sharp-scented branches brushed against his clothing, forcing Alec to lean forwards in his saddle as they forged their way through. Spotting a lighter area, Alec steered his horse towards it, breaking into a trot as they reached a patch where the trees were thinner. He could still hear voices back at the bandits' camp, fainter now, but he was sure that the whole camp was wakening. Alec saw more open ground nearer the creek and used it to speed up. There was a lot of snow cover, reflecting the star light and giving better visibility.

They came clear of the trees and the horses stretched out into a gallop. Tense as he was, there was something exhilarating in galloping through the snow under the stars. Lacey drew to his right, to avoid the snow being kicked up by his horse, but stayed a length behind. There was another patch of trees ahead before they reached the mouth of the gulch. A glance over his shoulder reassured Alec that no one was in sight behind them yet. He settled into his saddle and

61

studied the trees ahead, looking for a way through. Then Moray's head and shoulders seemed to disappear in front of him and Alec was flung off his horse.

He twisted as he fell, landing on his back in an explosion of snow that was in his ears, down his neck and up his sleeves. His horse lurched and scrambled past him, snorting as its hoofs flung clumps of snow across him. Alec could do no more than gasp for a few moments, shocked by the suddenness and the cold. Getting his breath, he floundered in the snow for a few moments before scrambling to his feet. There was a hole in the snow where it had been covering a narrow channel in the ground, a tiny creek bed. Turning, Alec saw that Lacey had passed him and was reaching Moray, who had halted of his own accord. She caught his trailing reins and led him back.

Alec shook himself and wiped away snow as he anxiously watched his horse move. Thankfully Moray seemed to be sound.

'Are you all right?' Lacey asked, as she handed the reins back to him.

'Aye,' Alec answered shortly. He pulled his glove off and examined his horse's legs as best he could in the dim light. 'I was a fool,' he said reproachfully.

Lacey looked back the way they'd come. 'We'd better keep moving.'

Alec patted his horse and climbed back into the saddle. He walked at first, a knot of worry in his stomach which gradually unwound as the horse continued to step out well. He seemed to have got away with his recklessness, but the accident sobered him.

Fleeing through the snowy mountains at night seemed like the height of foolishness. They depended so much upon their brave, vulnerable horses. Yet, since the moment Jason Alcott had hauled Lacey Fry from her seat on the train, he'd had no choice. He couldn't afford to brood about it now. Satisfied that the horse was all right, Alec pushed on to a steady jog, his eyes scouring the ground ahead.

They made it safely into the next patch of trees before any pursuit emerged from the woods behind them. The outlaws would have to scramble out of bedrolls, pack and ready the horses before beginning their pursuit, but his fall had wasted some of that valuable time. Alec still slowed to a walk as they wound their way through the trees. It was infuriatingly slow, and Lacey gave little whimpers of nervousness now and again. At last the light brightened again as they cleared the trees and saw the mouth of the gulch and the wide park ahead.

This time Alec kept the pace to a slow jog. He angled towards the creek, which was quite broad here, and flowing fast. The banks were overhung with snow in places, so he didn't get too close. Moving now at a brisk walk, Alec followed the creek downstream towards the river. Frustration grew as he searched for somewhere to cross safely. There had to be a trail, that would indicate the crossing point, but in the dark, and with the patches of snow, he couldn't find it. Trying to ride across in the dark without knowing where it was safe was foolish, as was trying to jump it. As he stared across the rushing water, his horse slowed of his own accord, lowering his head. Alec immediately switched his attention to the ground ahead. The snow was thin here but as Moray walked on slowly, Alec could tell he was moving onto softer ground.

'Back,' he said, for Lacey's benefit. He backed Moray until they were on firm ground again, glanced back towards the gulch, then looked over the creek to the park beyond and the pass over the mountains.

'We can't cross,' he said, his voice tight with frustration. 'Not in the dark.'

Lacey also looked back along the park. 'How are we going to get back to that pass? We can't wait here for daylight, and let them catch up with us.'

'We must go north,' Alec said. 'We must keep moving. Leadville's north of here anyway; we'll find another way across.' He had no idea where, and the failure of yesterday's attempt to cross the mountains was in his mind, but the wilder part of him, his Highland warrior half, his mother had called it, was roused by the challenge.

His mind made up, Alec turned his horse and set off at a steady jog. The mountain park was fairly open, with minor undulations in the ground. It was a little lighter on the other side of the river, as the rising sun touched the mountains there, but the side they were on was still dark and shadowed. Alec concentrated on the ground ahead, but Lacey must have been looking back from time to time. They'd gone nearly half a mile from the creek when he heard her gasp.

'Sheriff! I saw them, I'm sure I did.'

'Where?'

'Just coming out of the mouth of that gulch.'

Alec turned in his saddle to look, and spotted dark shapes moving across a patch of snow. As he looked, he saw Lacey, behind and to his right, kick her horse on. Alec swiftly kneed his horse across her path.

'Hold your pace,' he ordered.

'They're chasing us!' Her voice was close to panic as she reined back to a jog.

'We've got a good head start.' he reminded her. 'We let them run until they get close, using up their horses, then we speed up. It'll be lighter then an' safer. Their horses will have run a mile before they get within shooting range, if one of them doesn't hit a hole in the snow.'

'All right,' Lacey replied tersely.

The chase went as Alec predicted. When the bandits closed to just within pistol range, he speeded up until the distance widened again, then slowed back to a steady jog. The chasers gradually closed the gap again and once more, Alec and Lacey pulled away. It was hard riding, and as the sun rose, Alec was glad that their side of the park was still mostly in shadow. They slowed again, and this time it took a little longer for the bandits to close the gap. As they crested a rise in the ground, Alec glanced back. O'Leary had pulled ahead of the others, either impatient for the chase to end, or keen for the fight. Either would be typical of his impulsive nature. As they started down the other side of the slope, Alec urged his horse into a full on gallop.

It wasn't a very steep slope, but the gallop down was

exhilarating, not least because of the patches of snow that possibly concealed hazards. Alec was grinning as he glanced across at Lacey to see how she was coping. Her expression was determined, as she clung to the saddle horn with one hand, relying completely on her horse to carry her safely. They thundered down, taking the tiny creek at the bottom in their stride, and charged up the other side. Alec risked a glance back; no one was in sight yet.

'I'm going to stop in a moment; keep going,' he called across.

Lacey glanced at him, her face set and anxious, then nodded.

Alec sat deep and felt his reins, warning his horse before giving the signal to halt. Moray slid to a grass-tearing half, snorting as he did so. Alec turned him with his legs, wrapping the reins around the saddle-horn with one hand while drawing the rifle from its boot with the other. Putting the rifle to his shoulder, he marked the spot where they had crested the slope and aimed for it. Moray snorted once more, sucking in deep breaths as they waited.

CHAPTER SIX

O'Leary breasted the rise exactly where Alec expected him to. The outlaw saw him and whooped eagerly, kicking his horse onto greater speed as they began the descent. Alec waited calmly, letting them take three strides. It was enough time for the horse to be stretching out into a gallop on the downhill slope, but not quite enough time for the reckless O'Leary to recognise and react to the threat of Alec's rifle. As O'Leary began to haul on his reins to gather his horse together, Alec started firing.

Three quick shots, Moray's ears flickering with each one, though the horse remained still beneath him. O'Leary's horse shied and tumbled, throwing its rider off. Man and horse rolled downslope amid sprays of snow. To Alec's relief, the horse got its feet under itself and began to struggle up again. O'Leary also halted himself, floundering in a patch of snow. Alec threw another shot at him, and was satisfied to see the bandit collapse back into the snow, though still thrashing around and bellowing in pain.

He couldn't afford to wait any longer. Thrusting the rifle back into its boot, Alec unshipped his reins, turned his horse and started off up his side of the dip. When he reached the crest, he saw Lacey, some distance ahead. She had halted and half-turned her horse to look back, poised ready to flee. Alec swung his arm in a circle, indicating she should start moving. Lacey went on again at a jog, glancing back now and again until Alec caught up with her. She increased the speed of her horse to match his and they went on at a fast lope.

'What happened?' she called, her eyes searching him.

'I put O'Leary down,' Alec replied. 'I didn't kill him but he's hurt.'

'Good,' Lacey said firmly. 'You reckon they'll leave him or stop to tend to him?'

'They'll stop,' Alec said. 'They can follow our trail.'

Lacey nodded. 'But we've won an advantage?'

'Yes.'

Lacey didn't say anything else; she simply turned her face to the way ahead and rode.

At the sound of the gunfire up ahead, Alcott and his men drew their rifles.

'Spread out,' Alcott ordered, as they raced to the edge of the dip.

They breasted the rise in a rough line, eyes searching the land ahead. O'Leary's bay threw up its head and trotted away, leaving O'Leary sitting on the ground, clutching his left arm. Turner was gone.

'Slow,' called Alcott, not wanting to spook the loose horse more. 'Hannigan, go catch O'Leary's hoss.'

As Hannigan moved on at a trot, calling to the bay, Alcott and the other two halted near the fallen man and dismounted. Alcott didn't bother telling off O'Leary for his recklessness; it never made any difference.

'Bastard was waiting for me,' O'Leary complained, as Houston began examining his wounded arm. 'Son of a bitch just sat on that slope, waiting.'

'While you rode straight into his ambush,' Houston remarked. 'You hurt anyplace else?'

'Nah,' O'Leary said defiantly. There was snow on his fair hair and his clothes were rucked up from his fall. He sported a raw graze across the knuckles of his right hand but the rather wispy-looking man was as full of energy as a taut wire.

'Hoss seems to be sound,' announced Hannigan as he rode back, leading O'Leary's mount.

'Good. Then let's light a shuck after them.' O'Leary began struggling to his feet.

Alcott put his hand on O'Leary's shoulder and pushed him back down again. 'That arm needs bandaging,' he said firmly. 'There ain't no need to rush so. Turner can get ahead of us but he can't lose us easily and besides, he's got that girl riding with him. For sure, she's going to slow him down. And you'll be slowing us down iffen you're bleeding like a stuck pig.'

Leaving Houston to get on with tending to O'Leary, Alcott moved to stand by his horse, stroking its neck as he thought about Turner. The man was smart, Alcott knew that. He seemed to have given up on heading east into the Arkansas River valley and was going north, probably back to the territory he knew best to hole up. That's what Alcott himself had been planning to do. They just had to follow him north for a while and sooner or later they'd catch up with man who'd betrayed them and killed Jacob.

Alec and Lacey travelled steadily until almost noon, when Alec called a halt to rest. There was no sign of the bandits behind him, but he still chose a place where they could be concealed among trees, with a view a fair way back along the park. The horses were unsaddled and tended to before Alec joined Lacey to eat. She was in a small clearing where the sun was filtered through dappled shade. It was clear of snow, and when Lacey had finished her cheese and crackers, she lay back and stretched out on the grass.

'This feels good,' she said quietly, almost to herself.

'You've done a lot of riding,' Alec commented.

'Mmmm.' Lacey closed her eyes and relaxed.

Alec drank some more water, then decided to stretch out also. He lay on his back, enjoying the chance to let his muscles relax. It was very quiet. He could hear the river, not far away, and the sound of the horses grazing. Birds sang extravagantly in the trees around them. Alec had just let his eyes close when a soft sound from Lacey made him roll on his side to look at her. She was asleep, a few stray tendrils of her wavy hair dancing on the light breeze. A sudden jolt of adrenaline hit Alec: he'd almost fallen asleep himself!

He got to his feet before he could think about how much he wanted to lie in the sun and sleep. Once up, he made himself walk up and down. Alec stopped by the horses, talking quietly to them as he stroked them and rubbed their ears. The patient, peaceful animals were soothing and Alec let himself relax mentally as well as physically, while in their presence.

After a little while, he moved back towards the edge of the trees and found an outcrop where he could sit and watch their backtrail. Sure enough, it wasn't long before a group of riders came into view out of a fold in the ground. They were too far away for Alec to be quite sure of how many there were, as he knew the bandits had the two packhorses with them. They were moving at an unhurried jog, which told him something.

As he'd said to Lacey, they were leaving a trail which Manford, at least, could follow without too much trouble. They were at the top end of the park now, where the wide, grassy valley bottom narrowed to a gulch. They'd passed another couple of side gulches, leading east and possibly to passes over the mountains that divided them from the Arkansas valley where Leadville was, but Alec hadn't wanted to risk another dead end like the one he'd followed the day before.

Heading north was now his only realistic option, and Alcott knew that at least. Alec reconsidered his plans. To get to Leadville, he would have to travel north east, and then south again, skirting the range of mountains that divided this valley from the one to the east, where Leadville was. If he kept going east instead of turning south, he should be able to cross the mountains and head for Georgetown and reach the Colorado Central Railroad, which would take them to Denver. There would be telegraph offices along the railroad, where he could send a wire to Lacey's relatives too. Thinking as a lawman, Alec forgot that the bandits believed him to be an outlaw too, and didn't expect that he would be trying to get Lacey to the safety of a big town.

'Leadville's quicker an' easier tae get to,' he mused. 'They'll expect me to go there. So I'll do what they don't expect. We'll make for Georgetown.'

Alec studied the riders for a few moments, expertly gauging their speed and distance and picked a landmark between himself and them. Moving to sit with his back against a tree trunk, he simply relaxed for a few minutes until the riders reached that landmark. Only then did he rise, and return to wake Lacey and saddle the horses.

They continued on at a steady, economical jog, leaving the park behind. As the afternoon progressed, the soaring mountains on their right gave way to lower, more rounded peaks, scoured clear of snow in many parts. Not wanting to make things too easy, Alec waited for an area where there was plenty of bare ground, and turned up one of the valleys, heading north east. He guessed Manford would be able to follow them, but at least they weren't leaving a trail as obvious as it would be in snow.

They were much lower here, out of the thinner air,

and able to keep up a good pace.

'This looks more like New England,' Lacey remarked as they jogged along. 'The ground's rockier, and the grass is sparser, drier. But there's more deciduous trees here. The mountains aren't . . . looming over you in the same way.'

'Aye,' Alec agreed. 'It's a different feel, though we've not travelled very far.'

Lacey considered for a few moments, looking around. 'I like it,' she said decidedly. 'It's not as majestic as the high mountains, but it's still scenic.'

'Colorado's a beautiful state, for sure,' Alec said.

'What are those flowers?' Lacey asked, pointing to some low-growing plants with star-shaped white flowers that were growing near a patch of snow.

'Springbeauty,' Alec told her. He halted his horse and dismounted. Lacey stopped too, and watched as he unsheathed his knife and began digging up some of the plants. 'The corms are edible,' he told her. 'We can eat them raw or cooked. It'll make a change to have fresh food. I should have thought of it earlier.' He gathered a number of the small roots, brushing the loose soil off before tucking them into his jacket pockets. After cleaning and sheathing his knife, Alec pulled off a few of the leaves. He popped one into his mouth and chewed it.

'They're no' bad,' he said to Lacey, as he approached and offered her one.

She took it somewhat apprehensively, looked at Alec, who had started on another one, and tried hers. 'A bit like eating lettuce,' she decided, and held her hand out for another leaf. 'It is nice to have something fresh.'

The few leaves were soon eaten, and Alec transferred the corms to his saddle-bag.

As they travelled on, Lacey asked more questions about the plants and animals of the area. Alec answered as best he could, initially pleased to find something that kept her spirits up, then becoming pleasantly distracted from worry himself. He could never entirely forget the situation though; a part of him was always on alert to their surroundings.

It was Alec who first noticed the dark clouds gathering later in the afternoon. He said nothing at first, pressing on through the hills. Within an hour, Lacey was also casting anxious glances at the sky, and the temperature had dropped. The little creek they were following flowed into a valley running roughly north west to south east. Ahead and to the east were snow topped peaks, difficult to pass at present, but impossible after the snow fall that was coming. The only realistic option was to follow the valley to the north west, where the peaks declined, and to try finding their way around to the north and east again.

'We'll set up camp earlier today,' Alec said. 'Get ourselves some shelter.'

'How much snow will there be?' Lacey asked quietly.

'Enough.'

They rode for another half hour, to a point where the valley was beginning to widen out into a smooth, grassy plateau. Alec picked a spot on the lee side of a small gulch on the east of the valley. Lacey watched with interest as Alec edged his horse close to the trunk of a slender pine. He had to duck slightly as the lower boughs brushed his hat, but Alec soon had his knife out and began attacking the trunk, cutting and chopping it about his shoulder level. His knife was no way big enough to cut through the trunk, but Lacey kept quiet and watched, confident that he knew what he was doing. After a few minutes hard work, Alec had made a distinct gash in the trunk. Sheathing his knife, he unfastened a short length of rope from his saddle and tied one end around the trunk, above the cut; the other end he fastened to his saddlehorn. Dismounting, he took hold of the reins near the bit and urged Moray forward. The horse started forward obediently, lowering its head and pulling until the tree suddenly cracked and bent, showering snow from its higher branches. Alec immediately halted his horse, unfastening the rope and leading it away from the broken tree.

The top section of the pine hadn't broken off entirely, but the tip rested on the ground, some ten feet from the base of the trunk. Alec handed his reins to Lacey and drew his knife again.

'Watch this,' he instructed, pushing in amongst the branches of the fallen part. He hacked partway through an upward pointing branch where it joined the trunk and bent it down so the end touched the ground to the side. The air was rich with the resinous scent of pine as Alec fractured a couple more branches in the same way.

'Do you see what I'm doing?' he asked. 'We need to bring the upper branches down to form the sides of the shelter, and the branches underneath have to be cut off, to make space inside, and woven in to the sides to make them better.'

'I understand,' Lacey said brightly, cheered at the thought of having some kind of shelter to keep the snow off.

'Will you work on the shelter while I see to the horses?' Alec asked. 'Don't break the branches right through; just cut them enough so they bend.'

She nodded confidently and reached for the knife. 'I haven't built a den since I was nine, and this is much better than those were.'

Alec chuckled, and giving her the knife, led the horses to the creek to water them.

When he'd settled the horses under a neighbouring tree, Alec helped Lacey finish the shelter off with a floor of small, springy branches as insulation.

'We'd better hurry,' she said. 'If we're going to build another one before dark, and get a fire going too.'

'Another shelter?' Alec asked, straightening his hat.

'Well, you'll need one, too . . .' Her eyes widened, as she looked first at him, then at the small shelter. 'You plan for us to share that?'

Alec's curious look turned to a glare: he'd risked his life to save this girl from men who would rape her without a second thought and yet she didn't trust him? 'There's no' enough time to build another one,' he said tartly. 'An' I intend to sleep inside a shelter tonight, so you share it or you sleep outside.'

'I . . . er. . . .' Lacey wrapped her arms tightly around herself.

Her vulnerable look pricked Alec's conscience and the flare of indignation passed.

'I'm sorry, lassie,' he said more gently. 'I know it's not proper, but we'll each be in our own bedroll, and in any case, it'll be warmer with two people inside. I swear on my honour I'll not touch you.'

Lacey sucked in a deep breath. 'Of course, Sheriff. I know you're a good man. We have to be . . . practical, in this weather. I trust you,' she added quietly but clearly.

Alec nodded. 'Good. Let's get on.'

Soon after they ate, Alec wriggled himself down into his bedroll and looked up at the roof of green boughs low overhead. There was barely enough space for himself and Lacey in the shelter, but with a layer of leafy branches as insulation under the bedrolls, and snow settling on the roof, it promised to be a warmer night's rest than for the last few nights.

'I feel downright comfortable,' said Lacey, snuggling into her quilts. 'And those roots did make a nice change in the stew, didn't they?'

'I should've thought of them earlier,' Alec said mildly. He was more relaxed than he'd felt in days. Though the roof was only pine boughs woven together, it was still a roof and was keeping the snow off. The saddles and packs were tucked tight around the base of a nearby tree, where they were sheltered, and the horses were huddled beneath another. He and Lacey were both comfortably full of hot stew and coffee. With vague thoughts about the effect on morale of a full stomach and a warm bed, Alec fell quickly into a sound sleep.

CHAPTER SEVEN

The next morning, it didn't take long to leave the valley and reach a more open area where three valleys came together.

'A town!' exclaimed Lacey happily, looking out at the collection of lumber buildings gathered together between the surrounding hills. 'We can get help.'

Alec studied the settlement. 'I don't think so.'

'Why not?' Lacey protested.

'It's not got the telegraph, so we canna tell anyone where we are,' Alec explained. 'An' I don't think there'll be much in the way of law in such a small town to help us if Alcott catches up with us there.'

Lacey sagged in her saddle.

'We can go get some supplies,' Alec said. 'Get some sausage or beef perhaps.'

'There's bound to be a draper's store,' Lacey said more cheerfully. 'I mean, I know we need food, but seeing nice things again would be a refreshment after camping out like this for three nights.'

Alec chuckled and rode on.

Half an hour later they were riding along the main street of the sprawling collection of buildings. Lacey gazed about in wonder, never having properly seen a frontier town before.

'There's so many bars!' she exclaimed, looking at the saloon they were passing. 'But I can't see a school, or a church, I think. And it seems so noisy.'

'Aye, I guess that's a lumbermill up that way,' Alec said, pointing to the outskirts of the small town. 'And a quartz mill not so far away.'

'I can't see a draper's store,' Lacey said, halting her horse to peer across at the windows of a feed store. 'Oh!' she said again, seeing her reflection in the glass. She turned away and began combing her hair with her fingers. 'I'm such a mess, and so unladylike,' she said unhappily.

'Don't worry, lassie,' Alec said kindly. It was true that her long braid, with wild, loose corkscrews blowing in the breeze, was unsophisticated, and her walking suit was dirt-spotted and crumpled. It would hang oddly too, when she dismounted, with the supporting hoops having been abandoned days before. 'There's few enough women in towns like these that any woman's a treat for the eyes, and I canna think that anyone in this town will be in the new styles. You won't look so badly as you think.'

Lacey half-grimaced. 'You're very kind,' was all she said, but she carried her head a little higher afterwards.

They hitched their horses outside the general store

and entered, Alec carrying his saddle-bags. Lacey stared around at the crowded shelves and rails.

'I don't think I ever saw so many different kinds of things in one store before,' she exclaimed. 'Pots and groceries and tools and a stove and oh! I can see bolts of cloth and some ribbons over there.' She pointed to a corner half-hidden by shelves laden with tools, pots and ironmongery.

Alec saw the hungry look on her face. 'Why don't you look at the furbelows while I order the supplies,' he suggested.

She flashed him a brilliant smile and hurried off. Alec smiled to himself, and made his way to the counter.

Lifting the saddle-bags on the counter, Alec waited a few moments while the storekeeper finished tipping some striped candies into a glass jar. As the store-keeper put the lid back on the jar, Alec heard a man speaking elsewhere in the store.

'What can I get for you-all?' the storekeeper asked him.

'Two pounds of rice, please,' Alec replied, glancing about to see what else was available. 'And two pounds of those beans.'

'Travelling far in this weather?' the storekeep enquired as he began scooping rice from a sack onto the brass scales.

'I'm aiming for. . . .' He broke off as the voice of the unseen man suddenly rose, and was answered by a squeal from Lacey.

'Let go of me!'

Alec spun and raced to the far side of the store. Rounding the end of a shelf unit, he saw a burly man holding Lacey with one arm pinned to her side. She was beating on his chest with her other hand and averting her face as he lowered his head towards her. The big man grabbed the back of her head with his free hand and tried to turn her head to kiss her.

'Release her now!' Alec barked, as he ran towards them.

The miner glared at him. 'I saw her first,' he snarled. Dragging Lacey with him, he took a long, fast step to meet Alec, and swung a heavy fist at him.

Alec braked, swerved and ducked, narrowly avoiding the blow. He instinctively lashed out in return, hitting the miner's chest before stepping back. The barrel-chested man barely seemed to notice Alec's blow.

Alec held out his hands in a gesture of peace. 'Calm down now,' he began, though as he was speaking he noticed the smell of whiskey about the miner. His heart sank: he'd seen this situation often enough before. The miner was drunk enough to be aggressive, but not so drunk as to be easy to beat in a fight.

'Butt out, you runt.' Pushing Lacey away, the miner lunged for Alec.

Alec twisted and dodged, landing a couple of blows but mostly trying to avoid taking damage while he assessed the situation. The miner had the advantage of reach, weight and strength, plus whiskey-fuelled aggression.

'Stop it, you bully!' Lacey pummelled her small

hands against the miner's back. He grunted and turned to sweep her aside with his arm, sending her stumbling back along the aisle. Alec took advantage of the distraction to jump forward with a kick. He stamped his foot into the miner's thigh, rocking the big man. The miner reacted fast, swiping at Alec as he was recovering his balance. Alec was forced to skip sideways to avoid the blow. Still off-balance, a second blow was enough to send him staggering back into the shelves. Pots rattled as Alec collided painfully with the display.

Now he could see past the miner, and saw a second man coming to join the fight, pushing past Lacey as she scrambled to her feet. Alec grabbed the first thing that came to hand on the shelf, and flung a large saucepan at the newcomer. There was a satisfying clonk as it struck the surprised man on the forehead, and sent him to his knees. Alec had no time to congratulate himself. The first miner had got a hammer from the other side of the aisle and was about to swing it. Alec seized the next thing in reach, and blocked the blow with a large skillet.

The noise was earsplitting as they fought, the hammer ringing against the iron skillet as Alec defended himself. Dents appeared in the skillet as Alec parried with it, each blow jarring his arms and hands painfully. He tried to angle himself and the pan so the blows were deflected off as he was barely strong enough to stop a blow coming dead on. Catching one strike at the right angle, he twisted the skillet sharply and succeeded in briefly throwing the miner off-balance. As he caught his breath, Alec heard a clang, and glanced past his opponent to see Lacey with a dented pan in her hands, looking down at the second man, who was half-curled up, clutching his head. He grinned for a moment, before returning to the business of defending himself.

Alec deftly parried two more attacks, but the situation was untenable. As the miner drew his arm back again, Alec darted forward and rammed the edge of the skillet into the big man's stomach. The miner grunted and swayed back a step, swinging the hammer wildly. Alec just managed to catch it on the skillet, but the heavy blow jarred the pan from his hands. Instantly, he lunged forward, arms straight, throwing his weight against the bigger man. The miner was off-balance, and went staggering back, dropping the hammer. He crashed into a barrel of pick-axe handles, spilling them across the floor.

As he dodged the flying pick-axe handles, Alec noticed that both Lacey and the miner's friend had vanished. With a roar of anger, the miner seized a handle and Alec immediately did the same. Although he held it two-handedly, Alec instinctively fell into a sabre-fighting stance. The miner swung his stick in a hefty blow that Alec neatly parried. He riposted, jabbing the miner in the chest with the end of the handle. The pick-axe handles clacked together as they fought. Alec landed a couple more blows, but the miner's strength and aggression forced him to fight defensively. As he caught a hard blow with a classical high parry, Alec felt a momentary sense of the absurdity of the situation: duelling, but with pick-axe handles, not swords.

'Sheriff!' Lacey's voice came from the front of the store. 'There's more of them coming!'

The miner heard her urgent shout too. He grinned and went for Alec with a ferocious swing. Alec dodged backwards, forcing the miner to extend himself. Deflecting the blow high, he ducked under it and threw himself in close, holding his handle out straight. He rammed the end brutally into the miner's stomach, just below his ribcage. The miner gave a gasping shriek, crumpling breathlessly. Alec spun his handle and brought it down in a crashing blow across the miner's head. The big man slumped bonelessly to the floor, blood oozing from a gash in his scalp.

Dropping the pick-axe handle, Alec turned and sprinted to the counter. The storekeeper half ducked beneath the counter, staring at him with worried eyes. Alec took no notice: he snatched up his saddle-bags and ran to the door where Lacey was waiting impatiently.

'Mount up!' Alec ordered as he ran.

Lacey obeyed immediately, unhitching her horse and turning it so she could mount from the sidewalk. She was scrambling into her saddle as Alec burst out from the store. Angry yells told him which direction the miner's friends were coming from. The one he'd thrown the pan at was leading three others; they began sprinting as they saw him.

'Go!' he told Lacey, unhitching his horse's reins. As

Alec threw the saddle-bags across the front of his saddle, Lacey kicked her horse into a gallop. Moray threw his head up and snorted, but his training held and he stayed still as Alec vaulted aboard. Holding onto the saddle-bags and reins with one hand, and without his stirrups, Alec sent his horse leaping forward. Two of the miners jumped off the sidewalk, aiming to grab the reins or the rider. Alec drew his revolver and fired a shot just over their heads. One swore and ducked away but the other man stood his ground. Alec aimed directly at him. There was little expression in his face, just a professional determination. The miner saw the calculating coldness and changed his mind, backing away hastily. Alec swept past and fled down the street after Lacey, their horses sending clods of snow flying.

Half a mile out of town they slowed to a walk.

'I'm sorry,' Lacey said breathlessly to Alec. 'I didn't encourage him. He started talking to me and then grabbed at me.'

'It wasn't your fault.' Alec reassured her. 'He and his friends had been drinking and likely they don't see many women, let alone good ones.'

'Are you hurt?' she asked. 'I was so scared he'd hit you with that hammer.'

'I was worried about that myself,' Alec admitted. 'I'm no' hurt though. You did a good job with that pan, yourself.'

Lacey chuckled, her breath white in the cold air. 'It just seemed the right thing to do. Then he crawled away and I heard him shouting on the sidewalk, so I

86

went to see what was happening.'

'You did well.' Alec said. 'You can keep your head in a crisis,' he added approvingly.

She smiled, going a little pink, then glanced back over her shoulder. 'We didn't get any supplies, though. What are we going to do?'

'We've got enough to see us for a couple of days more,' Alec said. He halted his horse and dismounted to fix the saddle-bags back behind his saddle. 'We'll just stop at the next town we reach.' He spoke confidently, hiding the knowledge that he had little more idea of where the next town lay than Lacey did. Her faith in him was plain from her smile. Alec just hoped it was justified.

The rest of the day's travel was uneventful. After first continuing east, Alec turned northwards and forged his way across the hills and valleys. Lacey turned in her saddle now and again, but there was no sign of the outlaws behind them.

'Do you think they're still following?' she asked once, soon after they had started off again after lunch.

Alec considered for a few moments before answering. 'They will be,' he said simply.

Lacey didn't reply, just turned her face to the way ahead.

That evening, Alec took his time seeing to the horses, knowing that Lacey was gathering firewood and setting up the camp. He ran his hand through Moray's winter coat, then stood back to look at the horse. He'd just fed them the last of the grain, and had only made it last so long by giving smaller amounts each time. Both horses had been noticeably tired at the end of the day's ride and although Moray was in good health, he had a slight tucked up look that warned Alec that he was losing condition.

'Next town we see, we'll call in and get supplies,' he promised the horse. 'And there'll be a grand carrot for you, I promise, as soon as I can find one.'

The bay horse snorted gently and nuzzled him as he patted its neck. Alec smiled, and headed for the fire that Lacey had proudly lit.

There was at least enough food for the humans, if only bacon and beans again. They sat quietly by the small fire as the stew pot bubbled above it. Alec sat on his bedroll, warming his hands on his tin mug of coffee.

'Sheriff?' Lacey's quiet voice brought his attention away from the flames. 'You look a little sad – or thoughtful, anyway. Is something wrong?'

Alec smiled reassuringly. 'I was only thinking of my friends, my deputies. I've not seen them in weeks.'

'How long have you known them?' Lacey asked.

'Och, I've known Sam since we both first enlisted; we were bunkies when we first joined the regiment. Ethan got transferred to us a couple of years later, and Karl joined us when the regiment was being reordered, and I got promoted to lieutenant.'

Lacey stared at him. 'Enlisted, not commissioned? You joined as a private?'

'I did that,' Alec said simply, though he couldn't help smiling, pleased that she evidently understood his achievement.

'Two of my cousins went to military academy and they're both still lieutenants. There aren't so many promotions available in peacetime. How come you never went to a military academy?' Lacey asked.

'I never had the chance,' Alec said simply. 'Ma parents immigrated to America when I was six; we never had much money. They died in a fire when I was fifteen. I had to manage the best I could. I worked in a rail yard for a while an' I hated it. I enlisted to get out of the city – Chicago – as soon as I was old enough. I chose the cavalry because I liked real horses better than iron ones,' he added, with a slight smile.

Alec tended not to think about the years immediately following his parents' death too much. He preferred to skip from a contented childhood to the active life and tightly-knit bonds of the military. Being in the Army had suited Alec. He'd discovered both his ability as a leader, and a natural gift for military strategy. Just as important to his mind, he'd made some close friendships.

'The Army suited me,' he said. 'But I wanted to get back to a more normal life. I wanted to go on doing something useful and law work seemed to fit. I'm glad my friends chose to come with me; it wouldn't ha' been the same without them. The right company makes all the difference in a difficult job,' he added, a touch wistfully.

'I guess it does,' Lacey said sympathetically.

Abruptly setting aside his coffee cup, Alec leaned

forward to stir the stew.

'I reckon this is about done. Let's eat and turn in,' he said.

CHAPTER EIGHT

After a peaceful night, they set off again in a fresh, early morning. Following a creek downstream, it wasn't long before the smoke of a town came into sight. Alec smiled at Lacey, concealing his relief.

'Let's go get some food.'

As they rode along the street, someone left a restaurant as they passed. The open door let out a warm, savoury smell. Lacey inhaled deeply.

'Oh, Sheriff, couldn't we stop and get a proper meal, please? Fried chicken, or steak, with gravy, and a slice of pie, after?' she pleaded.

The smell, and her suggestions, made Alec's mouth water. He kept riding though.

'I'm sorry, lass; we can't spare the time. Alcott may only be an hour behind us, and we have to buy food for ourselves and the horses.'

Lacey sighed heavily, but made no objection.

They watered the horses at a public trough, then Alec moved on to a feed store. Lacey followed him inside, staying close this time.

'You want those filling?' the storekeeper asked, indicating the two small sacks that Alec carried. He looked at Lacey, looked harder, and smoothed fine hairs across the top of his balding head.

'Sure.' Alec paused beside one of the open sacks of oats and put his hand inside, stirring the grains up to assess them. 'I'll want a little extra too,' he added, satisfied with the quality.

'That's no trouble,' the storekeeper said, watching Lacey as she gazed about, examining the tins of molasses and blocks of rock salt. He switched his attention back to Alec, who was at the counter. 'I've got some small sacks in the back.'

Alec shook his head. 'I want enough to make two wee feeds for our horses, right now. I'll need to borrow a couple of buckets or dishes to feed them.'

'I sell things, I don't lend them.'

'The horses are right outside,' Alec said. 'We'll not be very long.' He put the grain sacks on the counter.

'I can sell you two nosebags,' the storekeeper replied.

Alec straightened, bracing to a military formality. Bringing out his law badge again, he slapped it onto the counter. 'Ma name's Alec Lawson,' he said, in the tones of an annoyed officer, with the glare to match. 'I'm a sworn Deputy US Marshal, and sheriff of Dereham County to boot. I need you to help me in the performance of my duties, in getting this young lady to safety.' His voice rang with authority. 'I need to borrow a couple of buckets from you,' he repeated.

The storekeeper glanced nervously at Alec, then at

the badge. He reached for the badge, as though about to pick it up, then changed his mind. He looked at Lacey, who stood watching, coolly waiting for him to make up his mind. The storekeeper looked at Alec once again, but could only meet his gaze for a few moments.

'I . . . er . . . I guess I can lend you a couple of buckets,' he whispered.

'Good.' Alec's voice was still firm. 'We'll get the horses fed, then fill up these sacks while they eat.'

The storekeeper nodded, and shuffled around the counter to start to pick up a couple of buckets. Lacey barely saw what he was doing; she was transfixed by Alec, who now carried himself with an air of command as strong as any officer she'd ever seen in full dress uniform and medals. If she'd ever doubted his story of rising to become a captain, she had no doubt now.

When the horses were contentedly eating, Lacey asked Alec if she could visit the nearby draper's store.

'I won't buy anything; I've no money anyway,' she said. 'But I just want to look at some lovely things again, and remind myself of what it's like to be all dressed up and pretty. I want to see nice, normal things again,' she pleaded.

Alec didn't really understand the particular appeal of a draper's store, but he got what she meant about wanting ordinary life and pleasant things. He nodded, and watched as she eagerly trotted along to the store and went in to enjoy the shelves of cloth and the ribbons. He sighed, without realizing. Ordinary, mundane, safe, comfortable life has ended for him more than half his lifetime ago, when his parents had died. He'd had to grow up fast to manage his life alone as a fifteen-year-old orphan. Then there had been the years in the army and in law work.

Alec had enjoyed his work, had enjoyed being able to help others, and, he had to admit, there had been times when he'd enjoyed the danger and the camaraderie it created with his friends. But it had never left him the time or the freedom to enjoy the ordinary sort of life. He'd been important as part of a system, as a soldier or a lawman; he believed he was important to his friends. But there was no one he was important to as family. The law building he shared with his friends was simply that – a building – not a home.

But he knew someone who was learning to make a house into a home. Lily, the Chinese girl he'd rescued from a group of moonshiners. Reverend Brown and his wife had taken the young woman in and Mrs Brown was delightedly educating her adopted daughter in the ways of being a good housewife. Lily was slender, beautiful and eager to please. She looked at Alec as though he could do anything in the world, and when she did, he felt as though he could indeed achieve anything. She'd been hidden away and abused by her former owners, and Alec delighted in showing her new things, and treating her to small luxuries. When she was around, he felt himself to be quite giddily in love, at last, and he relished it.

Lacey was back very shortly after the horses had finished eating and had settled down to doze, heads hanging low. Alec had returned the buckets to the feed store owner, who had taken them with little more than a formal nod.

'Oh, it was lovely,' Lacey said with warmth. 'So many pretty things, and they had the loveliest, green velvet, just the thing for a hat next winter.' She turned her head from side to side, as though showing off the new hat.

Alec smiled, and slung the saddle-bags over his shoulder. 'Come on. Let's go get some more supplies for ourselves.'

She nodded cheerfully, and followed him to the general store. Aware of time passing, Alec briskly ordered the supplies he wanted. Beans, rice, dried beef, raisins, cheese and more crackers were the first choice, followed by a few inches of cooked sausage wrapped in wax paper, by way of a change. He was adding a small tin of ground coffee to the pile of goods when Lacey spoke.

'Could we get some sugar?' she asked, pointing at the open barrel nearby. 'I do prefer it in my coffee.'

Alec shook his head. 'We've no tin to put it in, an' it wears through paper bags.' He saw her brave attempt to hide her disappointment. 'I'll tell you what though,' he suggested kindly. 'I could get some of that candy there, and you can dissolve that in your coffee to make it the sweeter.'

Lacey looked at the box of striped candy sticks on the counter. 'Oh, please, Sheriff. That would be such a treat.' Her smile lit up her sweet face.

Alec chuckled, and asked the storekeeper to put half a dozen candy sticks in a bag.

Once everything was paid for and stowed away in the saddle-bags, they mounted and were on their way again. Less than half an hour later, Bill Alcott and his men rode into the same, small town.

Alcott looked up and down the street carefully, but he didn't recognize any of the horses tethered there. Was Turner keeping out of sight or had he already moved on? Alcott looked at the stores, trying to guess what Turner would have done. He was getting tired of chasing this will o' the wisp; after all, he had the money from the robbery, little enough though it was. But the thought of letting Turner getting the better of him rankled. As well as making off with the woman, after all his protests about looking after her, Turner had killed Jacob. Alcott still felt numb about his brother's death; it didn't seem to bother him as much as he thought it should. He was angry about it, rather than sad. Either way, Jacob might have been a brash nuisance sometimes, but he was still kin. No one had the right to murder kin and get away with it. Besides, Alcott knew that his hold over his men had been weakened by Turner's actions. He needed to find and kill the little runt in order to keep his position as head of a gang.

'Lookee,' said Houston happily. 'I make out there's five saloons on this street. I sure could use a drink to settle the dust.'

'We're here to find Turner,' Alcott snapped.

'Aw, we've been on the trail for days,' Hannigan protested. 'I sure could do with visiting a saloon,

96

having a drink, seeing some pretty girls and remembering what it's like to be a man again.'

'Oh, yeah! Girls!' whooped O'Leary. 'I wanna see me some girls!' He snatched his hat off and waved it around his head.

Alcott mentally cursed Hannigan. He thought quickly. 'We probably ain't got time to do more than look at the girls. Turner ain't no fool; he'll be riding on.' he said. 'In any case, all the girls in a town like this will be as ugly as a tar-bucket.'

'But they're still girls,' O'Leary protested. 'I ain't seen a girl since Turner done stole that gussied up one that Jacob pulled off the train. And you wouldn't let us touch her none anyways.'

'Listen!' Alcott said sharply. 'Chuck, I want you to stay with me. The rest of you all can have 'bout half an hour in the saloons. You can have a drink and look at the girls, but nothing else, mind me? Turner killed Jacob and he stole that girl, after all that protesting that we needed to treat her good. So we gotta catch up with him, serve justice on him, and then, hell, you can do what you all like with the girl. It's certain sure Turner's already broke her in, so she's spoiled anyhow.'

O'Leary gave a whoop and kicked his horse towards the nearest saloon. Alcott caught Houston's attention.

'Keep an eye on him, Manny,' he said. 'We're moving off in half an hour. Chuck an' me are going to ask about in the shops, see iffen I can get anything about Turner.'

Houston nodded agreement, then sent his horse

after the others.

'I kinda got a hankering to spent time in a saloon, myself.' Chuck said, as they rode to the hitching rail. 'Be good to get out of this damn snow. Can't say as I'll miss seeing those three carrying on over the girls though, and by the time they've got warmed up, we'll be leaving again. It don't seem worth the bother of sitting down.'

They dismounted and hitched the horses, then lit cigarettes from the same match with the ease of long practice. Strolling to the nearest store, Alcott said

'Sorry we can't set a while and rest some, Chuck, but if the others get set down, it'll take time afore we can get going again. I don't want to let Turner and the girl get too far ahead of us, nohow.'

Chuck just shrugged and smiled, content to do as his friend wanted.

In the general store, Alcott explained that he was searching for a couple who had run away together and gave a rough description of Turner and the girl. The storekeeper said a man and young woman had been in not long since, but the woman had addressed the man as 'sheriff'. Alcott frowned at that, then concluded they must have been strangers. He bought supplies, then they left the store. Looking up and down the street, he wondered where else Turner might have been. The hardware store didn't seem likely and Alcott never even considered the drapers. He enquired at another general store, with no results and ended up back on the sidewalk. After peering in at the window of a restaurant, he looked round again.

'What about the feed store?' Chuck suggested.

There weren't many other places to try, other than saloons and hotels, and it suddenly occurred to Alcott that although Turner had taken some of the feed, he must surely have run out by now.

'Good idea.'

Moving decisively once more, he entered the store and simply explained that he was looking for a bearded man, and a woman. The storekeeper gave him a suspicious look.

'You ain't going to be asking to borrow buckets too, are you?' he asked.

Alcott shook his head, puzzled.

'Good.' The storekeep was glad to have someone to grumble to. 'Sure, he was buying some feed, but he wanted me to loan him a couple of buckets to feed his horses here and now. I wouldn't have done it, iffen he hadn't been a lawman.'

Alcott blinked, remembering what the other storekeeper had said. 'You're sure he was a lawman?'

The feed store man nodded. 'Pretty certain sure. I don't guess them deputy US Marshal's badges is too easy to get ahold of. 'Sides, he done claimed to be sheriff of Dereham County too. Called hisself Alec Lawson, and I seem to recall reading that name in the papers last year. Said as how he was getting the young lady to safety.'

'Did she look upset or frightened, like she was scared of him?' Alcott asked.

The storeman shook his head. 'If anything, I reckon she was kinda sweet on him, way she looked at him

99

from time to time.'

Alcott fought down the urge to curse. He took a couple of deep breaths as he considered his next actions. When he'd calmed down a little, he bought some grain to replenish their own supplies, and they carried it outside to load onto the packhorses with the supplies.

'You reckon Turner was really this lawman, Lawson?' Chuck asked.

'It looks like it,' Alcott grunted.

'Wow, he had us fooled all along. I guess it explains why he took care of the woman like that, sticking up for her and all. He must have had a conniption fit when Jacob wanted to bring her along,' he added with a chuckle.

Alcott jerked the straps of the packs tight as he worked, making the pack horse snort and stamp one leg. He didn't notice the look that Chuck gave him. Lawson hadn't just betrayed him by killing his brother and stealing the girl, he'd had him fooled all along. Alcott wrenched at the straps again, ignoring the protests of the horse. The other men couldn't learn about this! Being betrayed was bad enough; being made to look a fool was too much. Lawson had to die as quickly as possible, and the girl too.

'Don't tell the others about this,' he growled. 'Turner's still Turner.'

Simmering with anger, Alcott stalked into the saloon to round up his men.

Alec and Lacey headed east up a winding valley that

led into the mountains. Lacey chattered happily at first, relating her impressions of the little town. When they stopped for lunch, enjoying the sausage and the bread rolls that Alec had bought for a treat, she asked him about Lucasville, where he lived. He told her about the town, though he disappointed her with his lack of knowledge about the drapers and dressmakers.

The afternoon ride continued in good nature. The trail was steep, making progress slower than Alec liked, but he knew the outlaws wouldn't be travelling any faster. Lacey was more accustomed to the exercise, and to riding astride, which helped. As they wound back and forth along the valley, Alec kept a sharp eye on the weather; some dark clouds were brewing behind them. There was already plenty of snow underfoot in most places, and he began to suspect they were in for more.

Sure enough, by the later afternoon, the wind began blowing colder.

'We're gonna have to stop soon, to build a wee shelter,' Alec said.

Lacey turned in her saddle and looked up at the sky, taking in a deep breath of cold air. 'Oh, can't we go back to the town?'

'The town's nae good for us,' Alec answered.

Lacey halted her horse. 'I want to go back,' she said plaintively.

'It's too dangerous,' Alec said, puzzled at her sudden stubbornness.

Lacey looked about her, at the snow and trees. 'I'm fed up of camping out!' she exclaimed. 'I don't want to eat the same old thing, and sleep in my clothes

101

again or sleep on the ground. I want to be in a real house, with doors and windows and a roof. I want a proper bed and a stove to warm myself by, not a smoky fire, and oil lamps, and civilization!' By the end of her outburst she was sniffing, with tears gathering in the corners of her eyes and spilling over.

Alec was silent a moment, not knowing how to respond. He resorted to logic. 'We canna go back. Alcott and his men are behind us; we don't want to be running into them, lassie.'

'We haven't seen them in days!' Lacey protested. 'We don't know if they're still there. I don't care! I want to be indoors.'

She started to turn her horse but Alec's reflexes were fast and he grabbed her reins.

'Let go! You're mean!' She swatted at his arm.

'Silence!' he barked, as he would at a difficult recruit. Lacey's eyes widened in shock as she stared at him. 'We're no goin' back,' Alec ordered, his accent deepening. 'It's dangerous and plumb foolish. We have to go on to get to safety. That's my orders, you hear me?'

Lacey sniffed and nodded.

'Good, now we ride.' Releasing the reins, Alec gestured for her to take the lead.

Lacey set off in silence and Alec followed, unhappy and a little ashamed of himself. He hadn't intended to order her about, but he hadn't known what else to do. He didn't think he'd managed her very well. As a soldier, he'd spent many nights camping on the trail, but it was new for Lacey, and it had to be harder for a woman, he thought. They had no choice though, and if he had to bully her to get her to safety, then so be it. Alec just didn't look forward to it.

They travelled another fifteen minutes, Lacey maintaining her silence. Alec gradually became aware that a steady, familiar noise he was hearing was the processing plant of a mine, somewhere not too far distant. Looking up, he saw the smudges of smoke in the greying sky coming from the side of a peak ahead of them. It was little way off their trail, he thought, but not far. Nudging his horse into a fast jog, he came up alongside Lacey.

'You may get your wish to sleep inside tonight yet,' he said.

She looked around at him, her eyes wide with hope.

'There's a mine ahead; we may be able to beg shelter for the night.'

'Oh!' Her face lit up. 'Please, Sheriff, let's ask.'

'Aye, lassie.' He smiled. 'We will.'

Snow was already whirling in the air, as Alec stepped through into the little two-roomed cabin, and swiftly closed the door behind himself. The air inside was warm, and fragrant with the scent of beef frying in a pan, and something baking in the stove. Alec dumped the saddle-bags onto the lumber floor, and stretched before taking his coat off, luxuriating at being able to relax at last. He'd tended to the horses, feeding and grooming them before leaving them to settle in the mine's stables. His duties were done for the day, and Lacey was smiling as she came to take his coat.

'It's sure good of you to give us room for the night, Mrs Hodgeson,' he said.

The assayist's young wife was at the stove, prodding a pan of potatoes.

'It's no trouble, Sheriff Lawson,' she answered. 'We're both pleased to have fresh company, especially at the end of winter, when no one's been able to go visiting for months. It's lovely to have some woman talk, and hear about the latest styles back east, too,' she added, with a smile at Lacey.

'I declare, I hardly feel like a fashion plate,' Lacey answered, looking regretfully at her drooping and crudely divided skirt. Overall, however, she looked more content than Alec had ever seen her.

'It's quite a trip you're making,' remarked Hodgeson, a slender young man with a magnificent beard.

'Aye, an' Miss Fry's sure got grit, the way she's coped with it all,' Alec said.

Lacey smiled and flushed slightly at his praise. Mrs Hodgeson poured hot water from the kettle into an enamel jug and set it beside a bowl on a plain worktable near the stove.

'I'll fetch a towel if you'd like to wash up before supper,' she said.

'There's no need, thank you,' he replied, bending down to his saddle-bags. 'I can use my own.'

The warm water felt wonderful on his face and hands, making Alec realize just how much he wanted a hot bath and fresh clothes. He combed wet fingers through his dark hair, trying to freshen it a little, and used a little mirror to trim his beard as close as he could reasonably manage with scissors. Now that disguise was no longer necessary, he would have liked to be clean shaven again, but he'd left his razor behind when setting out as the bearded Turner.

The meal was good, all the better for being eaten at table, with the steady warmth of the stove and the shelter of wooden walls and a roof. Lacey was bright and happy, laughing more than Alec had heard before. After the meal, Mr Hodgeson played his violin and they sang a little. Lacey had a sweet, if somewhat uncertain voice. Alec had no great opinion of his own singing, but in fact was a pleasant baritone when he was coaxed into joining in. By nine o clock, Lacey was visibly wilting, and Alec was happy to turn in himself.

The cabin only had two rooms. It had quickly been settled that Lacey would share the bed with Mrs Hodgeson, while the two men slept on the floor of the living room. Alec smiled as Lacey decorously withdrew to the other room for the night. The last four nights or so they had been sleeping within sight of one another, almost touching one another while in the tree shelter he'd made, but now back in civilization, such a thing was not proper. It was good to have the freedom to strip down to his long johns and undershirt though, and look forward to a change of at least some clothes in the morning. Alec settled into his bedroll and quickly slipped into the deepest sleep he'd had for several weeks.

CHAPTER NINE

A sharp bang on the door woke Alec. He was half out of his bedroll and reaching for his gunbelt as cold wind from the opening door gusted over him.

'Hodgeson?' asked the shape carrying a candle lantern. 'It's Brown. Wake up!'

Alec had his short-barrelled Colt in his hand as the door was shut again. He couldn't immediately identify the voice, but knew it wasn't one of the outlaws. Hodgeson grunted and stirred among his blankets.

'Who are you?' Alec demanded. 'Why're you here?'

'Are you the marshal?' the man asked. 'Alcott's here, looking for you.'

Alec swore and scrambled free of his bedroll to stand up. 'How close?'

'He's at the staff house, where the manager, the assayists and clerks batch together. Morgan, the accountant is talking to them, trying to hold them up. I came to warn you and Cornie's gone to saddle your horses.'

Hodgeson was awake now, sitting up.

'Thanks for that.' Alec nodded to show his appreciation. 'Hodgeson, go wake the ladies. Miss Fry needs to be dressed and ready to leave as soon as possible, have your wife help her if necessary,' he ordered.

As Hodgeson stumbled toward the bedroom door, Alec paused a moment to think through the situation, and started putting his clothes on.

The light showing between the curtains of the parlour was the grey of early dawn. He recalled the layout of the mine buildings as he'd seen them the evening before. It was unlikely that he and Lacey would get far away before being spotted and chased. If they did escape unnoticed, the outlaws would search all the buildings. Once they discovered their prey had eluded them, they would be angry: Alec worried what would happen to Mrs Hodgeson. Not for the first time, Alec wished his deputies were with him; he was getting frustrated by always having to run, rather than being able to stand and make a fight. Looking at Brown, Alec began to consider his resources. Years of planning and fighting began to assert themselves as his mind worked fast. Tucking his woollen shirt into his trousers, Alec considered the layout of the buildings.

'Do you reckon you can reach the near bunkhouse without being seen?' he asked Brown.

Brown nodded, as Hodgeson returned to the living room.

Alec looked at the two of them. 'How many men there, fifty?'

'Near enough.'

'At least ten will own guns,' Alec estimated. 'Get

men armed an' waiting by the windows, and soon as Alcott and his men ride into the ground between the bunkhouse, this shanty and the stables, we can have them covered from two sides at least, three if we get someone armed in the stables. We'll be in cover, and have them outnumbered at least two tae one.' There was a dangerous look on his face. 'It's by far the best chance of stopping them altogether.' He turned to Brown, focused and full of energy. 'Get to the bunkhouse and wake the men, but keep it quiet. Have any with guns ready by the windows, but dinna let any lights show. We have to take them by surprise, understand?'

'Yessir!' Brown nodded, instinctively deferring to Alec's air of command.

Alec headed to the front window and peered cautiously through the narrow gap between the calico curtains. 'Don't shoot before a sign from me,' he ordered. 'It's clear, go.'

Brown made a rapid exit, crunching across the trodden and patchy snow to the nearest door of the bunkhouse. Alec wasn't happy about leaving the miners to wait in ambush on their own; once again he wished for one of his deputies to be present. He swiftly reconsidered his plans. The women would be safer in the bunkhouse, with plenty of men to defend them, and he would be able to command the men there. He spun to face Hodgeson.

'I want the women across in the bunkhouse. I'll go with them and send a couple of men back to defend from here, so we have Alcott surrounded.'

'I have a shotgun,' Hodgeson volunteered, somewhat uncertainly. 'I use it to hunt duck and geese.'

'Good.' Alec gestured towards the bedroom as he strode towards his bedroll. 'I want them moving out as soon as possible.'

Alec swiftly pulled on boots, vest, jacket and gunbelt, working largely by touch in the near dark. Hodgeson knocked and poked his head through the door, urging the women to hurry. Alec heard his wife's answer that they were doing the best they could, but it would take a few minutes.

'Light the lamp on the table, but keep it turned low,' Alec instructed. He picked up his rifle and moved to the window, peeping through the gap in the curtains before heaving the lower part up a few inches and propping it open. Bitter air came swirling in, sharp in his nose. Soft yellow light pooled in the centre of the room as the lamp was lit. Hodgeson stationed himself at the other window, copying Alec's actions.

Alec peered sideways between the curtains at the bunkhouse. It was hard to tell in the low light, but he thought that some of the windows were partly open; given the near-freezing temperature, he was sure that men had to be waiting behind them. He settled to wait, alert for any sound or movement, shivering slightly when icy air gusted through the window. Hodgeson kept shifting restlessly, his rapid breathing audible in the quiet. The only other sound was the low murmur of the women's voices in the other room. As the moments ticked past, Hodgeson cast increasingly

109

anxious glances at Alec, who remained outwardly calm.

Alec heard voices in the frosty air, just before the group came into sight around the corner of the lumber storage building opposite. He drew back the hammer of his Winchester, focussing on the horses and riders in the poor light. That was the outline of Bill Alcott leading, with O'Leary's rangy figure flanking and slightly to his rear.

'That's the place.'

Alec recognized Hannigan's voice from one of the shapes just beyond Alcott, and glimpsed the gesture towards the shanty he was in. Hodgeson twitched, tension radiating from his hunched shape. Still and silent, Alec waited until the group of riders was clearly in the space between shanty and bunkhouse.

'Halt!' he bellowed, in the voice of a parade ground officer. 'This is Deputy US Marshal Lawson. You're surrounded. Throw down your weapons and surrender!'

The group of riders came to a ragged halt, horses throwing up their heads in protest at the sudden pull on the reins. There were exclamations and curses from the outlaws. O'Leary's voice rose above the others.

'That sounded like Turner. Godammit, that was Turner!'

'Raise yer hands!' Alec barked.

'I hear him too.' That was Houston's drawl.

One of the horses moved forward slightly: Alec couldn't see if it was deliberate on the rider's part. The dim figures shifted, arms moving. There was a flash of light from one of the windows in the bunkhouse and the crack of a shot.

A ragged series of shots broke out; the crack of rifles and the deeper boom of shotguns as the other miners reacted to that first shot. Men and horses screamed as the group in the centre erupted into a whirl of confusion. Horses shied and plunged, dark shapes scattering and falling. More shots made a jagged drum roll, one or two coming back in return. Alec aimed for Alcott, but the outlaw turned his horse just before he fired and the shot missed. One horse fell, screaming and kicking. Another spun and bucked, tossing the rider, who fell limply and lay moaning.

'For God's sake, help me!'

As the outlaws turned and scattered, Alec saw a shape lunging up from beside the fallen horse. He fired, but missed again as the figure, Hannigan, from the voice, ducked aside. O'Leary screamed a mad defiance, firing his pistol rapidly towards Alec's window, as his horse danced on the spot. Glass shattered, and Alec ducked his head as shards pattered down into his hair and onto his back and shoulders. Hoofs thundered as horses galloped away, gunshots following them. O'Leary had stopped shooting. Alec started to rise, but hissed in pain and stopped, as glass stabbed deeper into the back of his neck. He hadn't felt it hit in the adrenaline of the moment, but now the sting was sharper and blood was trickling under his collar. A shiver of fear ran down his back at the thought of how close the glass had come to his spine.

The shooting died down as the outlaws fled, a few

shots and curses hurled after them. Alec lowered his rifle to the floor, careful not to move his head.

'Are you all right?' Hodgeson called.

'Glass in my neck.'

'Oh, wait.' Hodgeson hurried to the table for the lamp and turned it up, before bringing it over to where Alec waited. 'There's glass in your hair. Let me get that too before you move,' he said.

Alec winced as the glass was pulled from the back of his neck, then waited as patiently as he could while Hodgeson plucked out fragments of glass from his thick hair. He could hear voices outside, and what he thought were the low groans of the injured horse.

'I think that's about. . . .'

Alec rose, scattering glass from his jacket, before Hodgeson finished speaking, and took a couple of steps away before stopping to shake his head vigorously. With no more thought about the glass, he went outside.

A couple of lanterns cast pools of yellow light into the grey and white scene. The injured horse was Hannigan's black and white pinto, which blended with the patches of blood-dark snow on the ground. One man was crouched by its neck, another by its head. As Alec approached, there was the crack of a pistol shot. The horse shuddered once and ceased to move, its groans of pain silenced. Close by, another lantern shone warm light over Chuck Manford, sprawled limply. Alec joined the men who were gathered around the outlaw.

Manford was unconscious, blood from his mouth

gleaming darkly in his beard, and a larger patch of blood soaking the front of his coat. His breathing was ragged, bubbles of blood appearing at the corner of his mouth.

'I don't reckon he's gonna make it,' said one of the miners. He sounded as though he wasn't sure if this was good.

'That's Chuck Manford,' Alec said. He straightened up, addressing the men outdoors and the shapes visible in the windows of the bunkhouse. 'Wanted in connection with fifteen armed robberies, of stores, banks, trains and stagecoaches, and also for kidnapping. Alcott and his men have injured seven men, and killed two.'

'Guess he ain't gonna be no loss to no one,' someone said, and there were sounds of agreement from others.

'Take him inside and find a bed for him,' Alec instructed. 'He probably won't make it, but we should give him a chance.'

'America's a civilized country,' the man next to Alec said dryly. 'We don't leave even outlaws to die out in the snow.'

'There's women in that there shanty,' someone else said, indicating the Hodgesons' place. 'We don't want them looking out the windows and seeing a man dying out front. It might give them the vapours.'

There were grunts of amusement from the listeners. Two men picked Manford up and carried him into the bunkhouse. Alec got someone to help him free Hannigan's saddle-bags from the pinto's body, and carried them back to the shanty, after thanking the miners for helping him fight off the outlaws.

The women had managed to loosely fix a blanket over the broken window, and Mrs Hodgeson was sweeping up the shattered glass.

'Sorry about that,' Alec said, dumping the saddle bags on the table.

'Was anybody hurt?' asked Lacey, approaching him. 'Oh!' she exclaimed, holding a hand towards his neck, but pulling it back before she touched him.

'That's nae but a scratch,' Alec told her. 'I think it's the worst injury any of us got. One of the outlaws is badly injured; I don't reckon as he'll make it through the day.'

'Who was it?' Lacey tore her eyes away from the congealing blood on his neck.

'Manford. The tracker, who rode the brown.' He turned to Hodgeson. 'Send someone to the barn to unsaddle our horses, please. We'll not be leaving for a while yet; it's scarce dawn now, and we can all stand a little more sleep.' He opened the nearer saddle-bag and started to pull out the contents.

'You should have that cut seen to first,' Lacey said. She turned to Mrs Hodgeson for support. 'It should be cleaned at least, I'm sure. It could get infected.'

Alec saw the sense in her argument, and suffered to sit while the blood was cleaned away by Mrs Hodgeson, and a few neat stitches put in. By the time it was done, and everything tidied up, the excitement of the outlaws' visit had died down. They returned to the beds, and to Lacey's surprise, all fell asleep again.

*

It was close to mid-morning by the time breakfast was finished. Gubson, the mine manager appeared, and Alec thanked him for his support. Gubson accepted a mug of coffee gratefully, for the room was cold, even though the stove was well stoked and hot. The manager glanced at the flapping blanket over the window.

'I'll send you a tarp from stores,' he promised Hodgeson. 'You nail that down good and it should keep the wind out until we can get more glass brought in from Vail, iffen there's any in the stores there.'

'Will Georgetown not be better stocked?' Alec asked. 'It's on the railroad.'

Gubson shook his head. 'The railroad's been blocked by snow for months. There might be glass but it's no more certain than Vail. Besides, it looks like them outlaws went that way.'

Alec bit back a curse; he'd been aiming for Georgetown and the railroad, to deliver himself and Lacey quickly and comfortably to the safety of Denver. If the train couldn't get through the mountains, it would be a tough and dangerous ride on horseback. He sipped the strong, sweet coffee as he thought. East, to Georgetown, was nigh on impassable, and too risky, if Alcott had gone that way. Back west, to Vail, was pointless. South was Leadville, a large town, on the railroad, and Lacey's original destination. The outlaws might have started east, but there was nothing to stop them from swinging southwards, towards Leadville, and lying in wait at some point. Now they knew he was a lawman, it seemed reasonable for them to expect that he would head for the large town and its railroad. It was the logical thing to do, but it meant riding through country that Alcott knew far better than he did himself.

If he went north, he would be in his own county in a couple of days. He would have the advantage there, knowing it so well, and Alec couldn't think of any reason why the outlaws would expect him to head north, rather than south.

It took just a couple of minutes for Alec to weigh up his options and come to a decision. North it would be, the least obvious direction for him to choose, and therefore assuredly the safest.

CHAPTER TEN

Chuck was gone. The way he'd fallen from his horse told Alcott that he wasn't going to get up again soon, if ever. He was gone and that hurt. Seven years they'd ridden together. They'd worked it out back on New Year's Day, while sharing a cigarette between them because money had been low. Chuck hadn't beefed about that; he'd just smiled and got on with it, like he always did. They stuck together through the times they'd been so broke they'd re-used coffee grounds, and the times they'd had enough money to buy themselves the best whores in Leadville. It had been good to know that Chuck was there, steady and sensible; Alcott felt as though a rock had been taken away from beneath him.

In a moment he knew that losing Chuck hurt more than losing his own brother had, and that knowledge was followed by a surge of guilt. Alcott unthinkingly pressed his heels into his horse's sides, as though trying to outrun the guilt.

'Alcott, hey, Alcott! We gotta stop.'

The shout broke through Bill Alcott's self-absorption and the dark thoughts circling around in his mind. He leaned back in his saddle and tightened the reins. His liver chestnut dropped quickly from its brisk, smooth lope to a walk, stretching out its neck and swelling its sides with a sigh. Alcott looked at the other three men with him: three, when, what was just about a week back, there had been six. One dead, one lost, probably dead, and one a traitor.

Hannigan was sitting awkwardly in his saddle, his swarthy face pale and strained. That wasn't even his own saddle; he was riding Chuck's brown. Houston was riding Jacob's bay mare and at first glance, Alcott thought it was unusually dark with sweat. Then he realized that the dark patch on its side was blood, both its own, and Houston's as they had been peppered with buckshot. The packhorse he was leading was going lame on its near fore. O'Leary's arm was still bandaged after being shot by Lawson four days back, but he was sitting with his head up and alert, apparently refreshed by the fight and the gallop.

A look back along the valley reassured Alcott that they weren't being followed. He indicated a clump of pines not too far away.

'We'll make a halt there,' he said.

Though Hannigan and Houston were injured, the horses were seen to first. As soon as he could be spared, Alcott told Houston to find some wood and start a fire.

'Fix plenty of hot water,' he said. 'Make sure there's enough for coffee as well as fixing up wounds.'

The packhorse had sprained a tendon; it needed days or weeks of rest to recover. Alcott stripped its gear off and let it loose. When they were ready to leave he'd scare it away with a couple of shots and let it take its chances on the range. The buckshot hadn't hit Jacob's bay too deeply but it was weakened and stood with its head drooping as Alcott carefully cleaned the blood away and did his best to care for it.

'Houston, you'll have to ride the packhorse a whiles,' Alcott said. 'Least till we get to a town. This'n can take the packs for a couple a days.'

'Right.' Houston simply agreed, lacking the energy for anything more.

When the coffee was ready, Alcott produced a small bottle of whiskey and poured a generous splash into each mug. By the time Hannigan and Houston had been tended to, and the coffee drunk, morale had picked up a little.

'Turner,' muttered O'Leary. 'That was son-of-a-bitching Turner.' His voice began to rise. 'Deputy US Marshal, he called hisself!'

'Two-faced, low down bastard, is what he is,' Hannigan spat. 'He rode with us, and he's gone and killed Jacob and Chuck.' He winced at a stab of pain from cracked ribs.

'And took the girl,' O'Leary added, his pale blue eyes brilliant in the cold light.

Hannigan threw Alcott a challenging look. 'You reckon he's a lawman for real?'

Alcott nodded. 'The bastard's been playing us all along. Remember how he wanted us to go after a train on the Central Colorado Railroad? I just bet that was a set up to get the jump on us. He was flashing his badge to get the storekeepers to help him in that town we visited, and I bet he did the same at that mine. He owes us big time,' he added emphatically. He wanted the others to blame Lawson for their current situation, rather than thinking of his own mistake in letting the lawman join them.

'I want to see him bleed,' Houston said quietly, resting his hand on his blood stained trousers.

'I lost my good hoss and my kit,' Hannigan snarled, bunching his fists.

'Are we gonna ride back to the mine and get him?' O'Leary asked, gathering himself as though ready to jump to his feet.

Alcott shook his head. 'Ain't you got the brains God gave a flea?' he retorted. 'If we go back an' he's still there, we'll end up deader than beef. He's heading north, and we've gotta go that way too iffen we want to find him and pay him back.'

'Why north?' Hannigan asked.

'When he joined us, he told us he knew the area around Estes Park an' he weren't joshing us. Tur . . . Lawson's the sheriff of Dereham County. Iffen he was aiming for Leadville, he'd have turned south afore now; he's gotta be going back to his own territory. We can catch him before he gets there – cut off his balls and slit his throat, then take the woman.'

'Cut off his balls and hang him from a tree. Watch him dance whiles we take turns with the girl,' Hannigan said spitefully.

'I wanna see the girl dance too, once we've had her!' O'Leary cried, thumping the ground beside himself in his excitement. 'I ain't never seen a woman hang; I bet her titties surely do bounce while she's wriggling at the end of the rope.'

Alcott kept his face still, not registering his feelings at O'Leary's talk. But while the others were thinking about what they wanted to do to Lawson and the girl, they weren't asking how Alcott knew that Lawson was the Dereham County sheriff, and when he'd found out.

'We'll rest up here a while,' he announced, making the decision so naturally that the others didn't think to question him. 'We'll redistribute the goods from the lame packhorse so Manny's horse won't have to carry much, and eat something afore we leave.'

The others nodded. Hannigan and Houston lay back on their bedrolls, O'Leary started poking the small fire with a twig, and Alcott fell back into guilty thoughts about Chuck and Jacob.

Alec and Lacey left the mine about three hours after dawn. Chuck Manford had died a few minutes before they rode away from the noise and smells of the machinery, and the bustle of the mine. Lacey had been cheerful earlier, her spirits buoyed up by the small comforts of the shanty and the presence of female company. She stopped chattering at the news of Manford's death, and remained quiet. Alec looked at her now and again but couldn't think of anything to say. He headed for the river, following it east through the mountains in the same direction the outlaws had gone earlier. He was watching the traces of their trail carefully, keeping to cover where possible and halting now and again to scan the land ahead.

Once through the pass, Alec was relieved to see the outlaws' trail continued on along this valley, heading eastwards. He didn't know if they would attempt to cross the mountains to Georgetown, or head south-wards towards Leadville. Either was fine by him, as he planned to head north along the Blue River, and then north-east to Lucasville. After a short search, he found a section of the river that was narrow enough.

'I reckon we can jump across here,' he said. 'I'll go first, and remember. . . .'

'Jump exactly where you do,' Lacey finished, smiling for the first time in hours.

Alec grinned back at her. Studying the river for a few moments, and making sure his horse was alert and paying attention to him, he circled away at a jog. As he turned back, Alec pushed his horse into a lope, increasing speed to a gallop as they reached the last few strides. Moray stretched out in a great leap, the chilly water flashing by beneath them. For a few, glorious moments, Alec experienced the feeling of flying, poised lightly on his horse's back. Moray landed on the far bank with a grunt, cantering on with a light-hearted buck of celebration that made Alec laugh. He slowed his horse and turned to watch Lacey and the dun approaching in turn.

Lacey was concentrating grimly, but showed no hesitation as she pushed her horse on. It, too, leapt out boldly, keen to join its friend on the other side. Lacey grabbed the saddlehorn just as it took off and hung on, not keeping as well balanced as Alec had done, but staying safely in the deep saddle as the horse took her over. She lurched forward as they landed, but there was a smile on her face as she straightened up again.

'Oh, that was . . . exhilarating!' she exclaimed.

'Och, we'll make a pretty wee horsewoman of ye yet,' Alec promised. With a grin, he nudged his horse into a canter, challenging Lacey until she was laughing breathlessly with pleasure at the joy of the ride. When he slowed again, her good temper was recovered and they talked as they rode, and admired the scenery.

It was a little past noon when Alec called a halt for lunch. The horses were tended to, with Lacey helping out more confidently, even borrowing the hoof pick to scrape out her horse's hoofs under Alec's tuition. Alec built a small fire to brew coffee and Lacey sweetened hers with a small piece of the candy, sipping it with pleasure as she ate sausage and bread. Once her initial hunger was satisfied, she began to look about at the wide river valley and surrounding hills.

'Where are we going?' she asked.

'To my own town, Lucasville,' Alec told her.

Her round eyes widened. 'Lucasville? Is that on the way to Leadville?'

Alec shook his head. 'Alcott will be expecting us to go to Leadville. With the head start they had of us, they can turn southwards and hit us on the way there. We go north-west, and in a couple o' days we can reach Dronfield, and I can send a wire from there to my

123

deputies, to let them know we're alive and where we are. We can take the train from Dronfield to Lucasville an' you'll be safe there. Your uncle and aunt can come an' fetch you. I'll talk to my boss, the state marshal, and we'll see about tracking down Alcott. He's weaker now; if we can keep him on the run, we can wear him down and mebbe corner him.'

'So, more sleeping outdoors on the ground?' Lacey gave a resigned sigh.

'Aye, but we're on the home stretch now,' Alec reassured her.

CHAPTER ELEVEN

The rest of the day's journey passed uneventfully for Alec and Lacey. A lot more of the snow had melted here, but the ground was very wet and soft underfoot. Alec was pleased to see that the more generous feeds had improved the horses' condition, and that their mounts were not so tired at the end of the day in spite of the poor going. They weren't getting the amount of hard feed ideal for horses doing a full day's work and staying outdoors in hard conditions, but he was being as generous as he could with the oats. When they made camp that evening, Alec was as careful as ever to groom all the sweat from their thick winter coats, but without grooming so much as to remove the natural oils from their skin, which protected them. Moray butted his head against Alec, who scratched his ears fondly in return.

Lacey laughed gently. 'I see why you chose the cavalry.'

Alec smiled as he made his way back to the fire. 'I figured it would save me a lot of walking. I didn't reckon for all the mucking out and grooming, let alone keeping the horse's tack clean, as well as my own equipment.'

'You don't mind it though, do you?' Lacey asked shrewdly, pouring him a cup of strong, unsweetened coffee.

Alec nodded thanks as he accepted the cup. 'I remember we had an old garron on our croft, back in Scotland. A garron's a pony,' he added, at Lacey's look of confusion. 'She was a kind old beastie, an' I used to feel like a king, perched on her back when she went about the croft to her work.'

'You remember what Scotland was like?' Lacey asked.

'Aye. It was so different tae Chicago, where we settled, that all my memories of clean air, and green, growing things, and space, were kept separate. I've nothing but happy memories o' that time.' He looked out through the trees that surrounded the camp to the rolling lands beyond. 'I always reckoned those memories are why I like Colorado so much. When I retire from law work, I aim to buy some land here and set up a horse ranch.'

'You're planning to quit working as a lawman?' Lacey asked, surprised.

'Not any time soon,' Alec replied. 'But it's not a job a man can do for a lifetime.' He stopped there, his eyes changing at the knowledge that he could be killed in pursuit of his job, and never have the chance to retire.

Lacey saw his altered expression. 'I see. I guess you

might want to retire sooner if you got married, perhaps?'

Alec had a sudden vision of Lily, with her straight, black hair and curious, black eyes, so exotic and beautiful. 'Aye,' he replied rather abruptly. 'I guess I would.' Draining his mug of coffee, he got to his feet and went to the saddle-bags. 'We'd best be starting some supper,' he said briskly.

'All right,' Lacey answered quietly.

The next day, Alec took things at a steady pace. The horses weren't the only ones feeling the effect of their long ride. Lacey had woken grumbling about being stiff and sore after spending the night on the ground again.

'We'll be in Dronfield tomorrow night,' Alec promised her. 'You can sleep in a bed there, an' we'll take the train tae Lucasville in the morning, if you want.'

'What about the horses?' Lacey asked, patting her dun's neck. 'How long would it take to ride to Lucasville?'

'We could get there by noon, riding,' Alec said. 'Otherwise, there might be suitable space in a box car to take them by rail, or else they can stay in a stable in town overnight and one of my deputies can fetch them back the next day.'

'I like this horse. Do you think I could keep him?'

'He was Manny Houston's horse. I guess he's property of the state now, but I expect you could buy him from the state if you wanted him. He's a kind horse and you've not done so bad with him,' Alec added.

'I'll have to think of a name for him,' Lacey said, smiling fondly at the horse.

Her stiffness eased during the day, but towards evening it was plain that she was struggling. The long days in the saddle, often over difficult terrain, were taking a toll on her. Her youthful reserves of energy were running low, without the rest needed to replenish them. Lacey stubbornly made the effort to look after her horse when they made camp, but Alec had to encourage her to finish her supper, pointing out that she needed the energy. She turned in soon afterwards and was quickly asleep.

The following morning, she allowed herself grumbles of complaint as she pulled herself out of her bedroll.

'Feathers,' she remarked decidedly. 'I swear I'm sleeping on feather mattresses for the rest of my life. Even if it means becoming a bad woman,' she added with a touch of defiance.

Alec chuckled. 'I'm not sure if the hotels in Dronfield have feathers in their mattresses; more likely to be straw, I reckon. But I'm sure they do have mattresses.'

'So long as it's a mattress,' Lacey replied. 'And I can stay in it for as long as I want.'

Alec set an unhurried pace, concerned for Lacey. He knew that she liked riding, but he reminded himself that she was not only a sheltered Easterner, but a woman. He didn't know if the prolonged exercise of days of riding might harm her in any way, but he was feeling a little guilty over how much he'd been expecting her to do. She'd complained less than some of the recruits he'd trained, though, which Alec admired her for. The morning's ride was a hard one, winding their way up a trail to a pass through a line of mountains. Though the horses were crunching through snow as they climbed, the sun was hot on their backs.

At last, the trail reached its summit and Alec drew rein.

'Congratulations,' he said to Lacey, breathing deeply in the thin air. 'You've reached the continental divide.'

'Really?' She looked out, shading her eyes with her hand. 'You're sure?'

'Pretty much,' he reassured her. 'We're near enough on my own territory here. I reckon Dronfield's over that way.' Alec pointed to the north-west.

'Will we make it by this evening?'

'All being well.'

A bright smile blossomed on her face. 'Than let's go. I want a mattress tonight, remember?'

'An' I want my lunch. We'll stop when we reach somewhere suitable.'

Lacey laughed. 'I guess stopping for lunch is all right.'

Alec insisted that she sat and rested through lunch, while he tended to the horses alone. She didn't argue, but fetched some firewood before sitting down. Alec didn't hurry lunch, giving her time to recover from the morning's ride. The rest, food and coffee had the right effect, and Lacey swung herself into her saddle afterwards without too much effort.

She kept in determined good spirits for most of the afternoon, continuing to ask questions about the plants and animals they saw. She exclaimed over the beaver dams and lodges along the river, and was the first to spot a herd of mule deer, that bounded away in long hops. As delightful were the white corn lilies and the yellow glacier lilies that spangled the grass. By the later afternoon though, the golden light faded from the sky as heavy clouds swelled up. Lacey looked at the dark sky, and sucked in a long breath of suddenly cold air.

'Is it going to snow?' she asked.

'Aye,' Alec answered. 'And soon.' He thought for a few moments. 'I'm not sure we can get to Dronfield before the snow sets in.'

She stared at him disbelievingly for a moment. 'But I want to sleep on a mattress tonight! Can we make it if we gallop?'

Alec shook his head. 'I'm sorry, lassie, that storm's coming on fast. We can hustle but you don't want to be riding when the snow arrives. If we're mebbe a mile or so from Dronfield when it starts, we'll ride on, but if I think we're too far away, we'll have to stop and make shelter for the night. There'll be no time for arguing, unless you want to sleep cold tonight.'

Lacey looked back at the thick clouds gathering, and gave an impatient sigh. 'All right,' she said tautly.

'Good lass; come on, then.' Alec nudged his horse forward into a steady lope.

*

The door to the saloon opened, letting in Eli Hannigan and a whirl of snow. He shut the door quickly and brushed the snow from his hat and coat, adding to the dampness of the dirt-tracked floorboards. Ignoring a greeting from a saloon girl with a shawl wrapped around her bare shoulders, he joined his friends at a table close to the stove.

'Are the horses all right?' Alcott asked, pulling out a chair for him.

Hannigan slung his coat onto the back of the chair. 'Warmer than we are, I bet.' He sat, and took the glass of whiskey that Houston pushed towards him. 'No sign of Tur . . . Lawson, and if he ain't made town by now, he ain't coming today.'

'What if he went to some other place, instead of this town?' Houston asked.

Alcott shook his head. 'I asked at the railroad depot. If he's following us, he'll end up here, in Dronfield, same as we did. If he went up the Blue River and turned east, he'll come by here, 'less he goes more north east and comes back down towards Narrow. But he'd then follow the railroad from Narrow down to here, to get back to Lucasville, so why bother? It's quicker to come directly here, and this is his territory; he knows his way about.' He drew deeply on his cigarette.

Hannigan grinned evilly. 'I sure hope he is camping out somewhere in this snow. Serves the Scots bastard right.'

'He's got that girl to keep him nice and warm,' O'Leary said.

'Yeah, she sure looked plump and ripe for the picking,' Hannigan replied.

'You reckon she's giving as good as she gets, or just letting him get on with it?' O'Leary wiggled in his seat to indicate what he meant.

Hannigan laughed. 'I like me a go-er,' he said, smiling loosely.

Alcott tuned out their conversation as it got lewder. He'd been able to ignore them in the past, because he'd had Chuck to talk to. A sudden wave of grief for Chuck struck him, and he took a deep breath, trying not to let it show. Alcott held himself very still until the pain eased up a little. He took a slug of whiskey, almost welcoming the harsh, cheap taste. It was poor whiskey because he didn't want to spend money on anything better; there just hadn't been much money from that last robbery. His grief and resentfulness found an easy target. It was all Lawson's fault. It was Lawson's fault that they were scraping by and it was Lawson's fault that Chuck was dead. Alcott took another sharp swallow of whiskey, drew on his cigarette, and lapsed into a daydream about confronting the lawman and shooting him down.

'Did you sleep all right?' Alec asked Lacey as she untangled herself from her bedroll under the low shelter he'd contrived the night before.

'Yes, thank you,' she answered, attempting to tuck stray corkscrews of chestnut hair behind her ears.

132

'These tree shelters do keep you warm, though it seems a shame that you have to break the trees to make them. All the same,' she added firmly. 'I'm expecting to sleep in a house, with a proper bed tonight.'

Alec chuckled. 'I'll do my best.'

They took a leisurely breakfast, eating generous portions with the comfort of knowing their hard journey was almost over. As soon as Lacey finished her coffee, she began to hustle, gathering up the plates to clean them in the snow.

'I'll see to these and the bedrolls while you get the horses ready,' she said briskly.

Alec smiled and gave her a salute. 'Yes, sir,' he answered crisply.

She coloured slightly but smiled back as she stood up.

Lacey had got practised at packing up the camp and they were soon mounted and on their way. The sun was already warm when they left, the horses crunching their way through the fresh snow.

'How long till we reach the town?' Lacey asked.

'Och, it'll not take an hour,' Alec replied.

She gave him a mock scowl. 'I bet we could have made it last night if we'd hustled.'

'You saw how hard it was snowing last night, time we got the supper cooking. You wouldn't want to be riding in that for half an hour or so. An' we wouldn't be able to go faster than a walk in that weather,' Alec said reasonably.

Lacey glowered briefly, then dropped the act. 'This

town, Dronfield, what's it like? Is it big, are there many stores, how old is it?'

'Half of it's a lot newer than the rest.'

'Did it grow a lot suddenly?'

Alec shook his head. 'Not at all. Half of it was destroyed when two locomotives and two cars of explosives blew up there last fall.'

Her eyes became circular. 'Oh my gosh! Really? Did you see it? What happened?'

Alec half-smiled at her amazement. 'Aye, I was there. The blast knocked me clean off my feet, too.'

Lacey listened, rapt, as he told her the story about a murderer he and his deputies had been chasing, and the train wreck the killer had caused.

When they reached the edge of the small town, Alec pointed out the newer railroad tracks, laid over the filled-in crater.

'I can see the difference in colour,' Lacey agreed. 'And the nearer buildings look pretty new, too.'

Alec took out his pocket watch and looked at it. 'If this is still keeping the right time, I reckon there's another couple of hours or so until the next train's due.'

'There'll be time to look around, and arrange things then?' Lacey asked.

'Aye, there's no hurry.'

The horses picked their way over the railroad tracks, and headed along the main street, leading away from the station. Lacey gazed about eagerly, letting her horse make its own way along the slushy street.

'Oh, just look at that darling hat!' she exclaimed,

pointing to the window of a draper's store.

Alec reined in his horse. 'Do you want to stop here an' look in the window while I go on to the telegraph office? I'll not be a few minutes, an' once I've wired my deputies, we can see about the trains.'

Lacey nodded happily, so they hitched their horses outside the draper's and parted ways. Alec strode a few doors along to the telegraph office and waited in line for a couple of minutes, taking the time to think out the message he wanted to send. He also checked his pocket watch against the clock in the office and was pleased to see it was only a few minutes slow. He adjusted it and relaxed, knowing there was plenty of time before the next train to Lucasville.

When it was his turn at the counter, it only took a minute or two for the message to be dictated, paid for and sent. Alec nodded his gratitude to the operator and left, feeling relieved at being able to get in touch with his friends at last. All he'd done was to notify them of where he was, that he had Lacey with him, and thought Alcott was in Leadville, but he knew his friends would be glad to know all was well. He'd had no contact with them for nearly a month, and worried about them, as he knew they'd be worrying about him.

Leaving the office, thinking of his friends, Alec nearly bumped into someone outside on the sidewalk. Neatly stepping back half a pace, he was on the point of apologizing, when he realized it was Manny Houston he'd almost collided with. Houston was equally startled, but it was Alec who recovered first.

CHAPTER TWELVE

In a flash, Alec realized that if Houston was in Dronfield, then the others probably were too; he had to deal with Houston as quickly and as quietly as possible, to avoid attracting their attention. Which meant he couldn't use his gun. Acting as fast as he thought, Alec caught his balance and delivered a powerful kick straight to Houston's groin. Houston gave a strangled yelp and folded, clutching himself. Alec swivelled and pushed him face-first onto the sidewalk, then delivered a sharp kick to his head. He bent, and was reaching for Houston's gun when someone yelled.

'Hey, mister, what the hell are you doing? Leave him alone.'

Alec looked up at the man: a stranger, and unarmed. 'Law business,' he snapped.

'I don't see no badge,' the neatly-dressed man called back. He was a couple of doors down from the telegraph office, out front of a saloon.

Alec mentally cursed himself. He usually wore his badge proudly for all to see. The last few weeks, he'd had to keep it hidden, but had never stopped thinking of himself as a law officer. He'd got out of the habit of wearing a badge and wasn't yet back in his normal life; the badge had slipped his mind. He couldn't be surprised at this officious man doubting his word.

'My name's Sheriff Lawson. I'm also a deputy US marshal.'

'Where's your badge then, Sheriff?'

After a quick glance at the moaning Houston, Alec unbuttoned the top of his coat to reach inside for his badge to display it. With his senses on high alert, he spotted movement in the doorway of the saloon where the stranger was. The door had opened slightly and something protruded from within, breaking the outline of the door. A brief glimpse was enough to warn Alec. He threw himself sideways, almost over Houston, and rolled across the sidewalk to drop into the snowy street, as the gun in the doorway fired.

Horses tethered nearby shied and snorted at the noise. As Alec scrambled to hands and knees, he heard O'Leary shouting.

'I got him. I got the bastard!'

Drawing his gun, Alec knelt by the sidewalk, using Houston as added cover. Houston was stirring, reaching for his own gun. Alec lunged to his feet and reached over him, grabbing the Colt. He heard O'Leary's shout and ducked back as a shot cracked

137

over his head. Houston yelled an inarticulate protest towards O'Leary, who was now on the sidewalk outside the saloon door, Alcott behind him. The interfering stranger had sensibly fled when the shooting started. Houston rolled away from Alec, towards the wall of the telegraph office, as O'Leary fired another shot. That one tore up a length of sidewalk, and set a nearby horse plunging and pulling at its reins.

Crouching beside the sidewalk, Alec fired fast shots with both guns. Houston's Colt was the Cavalry model, longer and heavier than the Artillery Colt he used. He knew he didn't stand much chance of hitting anything with it, especially in his off hand, but that wasn't his intention. He just fired a succession of shots back at O'Leary, who yelled, and dived for cover inside the saloon, which was all that Alec wanted at that moment. As soon as O'Leary was inside, Alcott yanked the door shut.

Alec put Houston's gun on the sidewalk and quickly switched fresh bullets into his own, all the time making quick glances at Houston and the front of the saloon. While he had his hands full, Houston staggered up and scrambled into the telegraph office. Alec cursed under his breath, but didn't waste time taking a shot at the unarmed man. He'd just got the last round chambered when he glimpsed movement behind the painted saloon window, and the glass was broken from the inside.

Without stopping to think, Alec ducked. Shots were fired from the saloon, leaving the smell of gunpowder in the crisp air. A horse tethered outside the saloon by its reins, pulled back so hard it pulled its bridle clean off, and fled, scattering snow from its hoofs. Alec picked up both revolvers again and crouched against the small shelter of the sidewalk.

'Sheriff! I'm coming!'

Keeping low, he turned and saw Lacey jogging up the street, astride her horse and leading his. She was keeping an eye on the front of the saloon, plainly trying to gauge whether the men inside could see her. Alec gestured to her.

'Keep close to the sidewalk,' he called.

Lacey obeyed, making it harder for the bandits to see her without showing themselves to Alec. He caught a flash of movement and ducked again as more bullets cracked out.

'Come and face us, you turncoat!' O'Leary yelled.

Alec didn't bother replying. He glanced again at Lacey, and signalled for her to halt. She pulled up, watching him anxiously. Alec made a circling gesture. Lacey stared at him for a moment, then began to turn the horses. Not wanting to wait any longer, Alec straightened and started throwing fast shots into the saloon window. Glass shattered and sprayed inwards. Alec thought he heard a yell, and sincerely hoped that one of the outlaws had been cut by the glass, just as he had back at the mine. He fired at different spots, aiming to cause as much damage and confusion as possible, to keep the outlaws pinned down for a few moments. Emptying Houston's revolver, he dropped it, holstered his own, and ran for the horses.

Lacey held them steady as Alec ran and vaulted into

his saddle. They sprang forwards together, before Alec even got his feet into the stirrups. He caught the reins Lacey tossed him and found his stirrups as they pounded along the street.

'Thank you,' he shouted to Lacey, leaning over his horse's neck.

She grinned back at him, half excited and half terrified. There was a yell from behind them, O'Leary's voice, and a flurry of shots cracked out. Lacey squealed and Alec looked over at her, anxious. She too was leaning forward as her horse galloped.

'Are you hurt?' he called.

'No!' Her face was flushed and her eyes bright.

A few more shots sounded but Alec had no idea how close they came. As they approached the end of the street, he began to change direction.

'Follow the tracks down,' he urged.

Lacey responded and they turned to race beside the railroad tracks along the valley, leaving the small town behind them.

They covered over two miles at a steady gallop before Alec really noticed the pain in his right thigh. He'd thought it was a bruise or ache sustained from his roll across the sidewalk into the street, but as well as the pain, he felt increasing dampness against his skin. Looking down, he saw bloodstains soaking his trouser-leg, and saw the bullet holes of a shallow wound. Cursing, he looked about for a sheltered spot. Not too far ahead was a strip of trees bordering a creek.

'Slow up,' he called, pointing to the trees. 'We need to stop there.'

140

They slowed to a jog, then a walk, giving the horses the chance to cool a little before halting. Alec dismounted, hanging on to the saddle to steady himself through the first jolt of pain from landing. The world spun for a moment and he lowered his head, breathing deeply.

'Do you think Alcott and the others will be coming. . . ?' Lacey broke off as she saw him. 'Are you all right?'

'Got caught by a bullet,' he admitted. 'Must have been as we were leaving town.' The dizzy spell passed and he was able to turn and look at her.

Lacey drew in a sharp breath then became practical. 'That needs cleaning and bandaging straight away.'

Alec agreed. 'We've no' got time to waste. Alcott will be after us soon enough.' He took a couple of steps forward, limping. 'We should let the horses have a quick drink.'

Lacey moved into his path. 'You're white as a sheet, Sheriff. You shouldn't be doing anything.' She turned to her horse and started to unfasten the bedroll. 'You rest. We'll get a temporary bandage on it to stop the bleeding, then I'll fetch some wood and you can start water to heating while I water the horses.'

Alec wanted to argue with her, but he was feeling shivery now, and knew she was talking sense. If he tried to do too much now, he'd only put himself in a worse position. As Lacey laid out the bedroll on a patch of clear ground, he rummaged in his saddlebag, bringing out a small hipflask. He took a couple of swallows of whiskey and tucked it away in his coat

141

pocket. Accepting Lacey's arm, Alec limped to the bedroll and lay down upon it. He watched as she tethered the horses to trees and loosened their girths, before picking up firewood and bringing it back to him. Alec started building the fire as she fetched more wood.

'I don't have material to make a bandage,' he realized.

Lacey added wood to the small pile. She thought for a few moments. 'Lend me your knife, please,' she asked.

Alec passed it to her, wondering what she had planned. She hesitated for a few moments, then took herself out of sight behind a pine and a tangle of leafless shrubs. A couple of minutes later she emerged clutching an item of fine white cotton, that Alec realized was a petticoat. As she started slashing it into strips, he asked.

'Won't you be cold without that?'

Lacey shook her head. 'I still have my flannel one.'

As she completed the first strips, he took them and bound them around his thigh. When he was done, he held out his hands for the knife and cloth.

'I'll light the fire and finish this while you water the horses; we can't afford to waste time. Just let the horses have a short drink,' he told her. 'They could founder if we let them have too much and then push them hard.'

Lacey nodded understanding and went to collect the two horses.

A few minutes later, the horses were resting and

eating a small feed, while a pot of warm water sat by the edge of the fire. With Lacey's help, Alec had removed his trousers and boots and lay on his side in his flannel long johns. She cut slits in the leg of the long johns to expose the wounds where the bullet had passed through his thigh. After gently washing the sticky blood away, Lacey peered closely at the wounds.

'I think . . . it looks like there's something in the wound?' She was puzzled.

'It'll be fabric from my underpants,' Alec said, his face grim. 'The bullet punches it into the wound. You'll be needing the tweezers from my housewife to get it out.'

'Right.' Lacey fetched the tweezers and peered closely at the wound. She took a sudden deep breath and held it, before letting it out in a sudden whoosh.

'It's got to come out,' Alec said, steadily. 'You've got a steady hand, lass.'

Taking another deep breath, Lacey cautiously probed the wound. Alec gritted his teeth and clutched a fistful of bedroll, but made no sound. After moments that seemed increasingly drawn out, she suddenly exclaimed.

'I've got it!'

Alec let out a sharp sigh. 'Good work.' He reached into his coat pocket for the hip flask. 'Pour a little of this over each wound before you bandage it up.'

Lacey did as he said, bringing a sharp hiss from Alec as the raw liquor stung. She put pads of petticoat material against his leg, then wrapped the bandage over the flannel underwear. Alec was still a little shaky, but felt much better once he had his trousers and boots back on. Lacey looked at him carefully.

'You lie here while I pack up and get the horses ready,' she said. 'It's for a fact, you need to rest it as much as possible.'

Alec just nodded and lay back gratefully, though he watched as she packed things away and tightened the girths.

'What are we going to do now?' she asked, unhitching the horses.

'Make for Lyons,' Alec said. 'We get there first and we'll have the advantage when Alcott comes after us. I'll raise a posse of men to support me.' He'd rather have travelled on to Lucasville, where at least one of his deputies would be, as well as the town's own marshal. However, Alec suspected that his injury would weaken him, making a hard ride impossible, and they had already lost time while he was being treated. With that in mind, he let Lacey help him up and over to his horse, ready for what he sincerely hoped would be the last stage of their journey.

The outlaws rode to the sound of cursing and complaints, though Bill Alcott was almost silent, not wasting his breath. Houston grumbled now and again about the pain in his groin from being kicked. O'Leary was stirring himself up with vivid descriptions of what he would do to the girl once they got hold of her. Alcott found his lust dispiriting and grubby, but made no effort to stop him. He wanted his men with him, ready to fight and to finish this mess.

144

It had taken them time to set off after the fight in the street. Hannigan and Alcott himself had suffered scratches from the shattered glass of the saloon window, and Houston had been inclined to whimper, rather than try to walk. They'd had to sort themselves out and get their horses ready, before hitting the trail in search of Lawson and the girl. After a short argument, the packhorse and bags had been left behind for the sake of speed. Alcott felt a dark, brooding anger: Lawson had cost him so much. He'd lost his friend, his brother and his pride. He had to pay Lawson back; he wanted him to suffer, if possible. When it was over, when he'd seen Lawson lying in the dirt, Alcott decided he would move on. He'd make his way to somewhere else, Montana perhaps, and forget about all this.

'Hey, look there.' Hannigan pointed to the left.

Alcott saw the tracks leading away from the railroad, left in a patch of snow.

'Stay sharp,' he ordered, turning his horse. 'Lawson may be waiting in those trees.'

The outlaws drew their guns as they approached the strip of trees. They weren't thick enough to make good cover though, and it was soon clear that no one was there. The outlaws halted and dismounted, looking about.

'They made a fire,' Houston said prodding the mound with his foot.

'Looks like something was laid out here, a blanket maybe,' O'Leary added.

Alcott's eye was drawn by a glimpse of dull red at the

145

edge of a snow patch. He knelt down to examine it.
'Looks like someone poured some water away here,'
he mused, studying the snow. 'Water with blood in it!'
he realized suddenly. 'We hit one of them, and most
likely it was Lawson.'

'Can't be too bad, though,' Hannigan said gloomily.
'He rode this far, and they've gone on again.'

'It's still a wound, and bad enough for them to stop
and tend it,' Alcott said. He felt a new burst of energy
at the sight. 'They can't be too far ahead of us now.'

O'Leary let out a whoop that made birds call in
alarm. 'I'm gonna get me that girl soon!'

'I aim to pay Lawson back,' Houston said. 'I want to
pepper him with shot and see how he likes it; some in
his arm, some in his leg. Let him stew and suffer for a
while, then put a load into his belly and let him lie
there and watch his own guts oozing out.'

'Then let's get going.' Alcott caught his horse and
mounted. 'I want this settled.'

They set off again at a brisk lope, enthusiasm
renewed. Hannigan and Houston ceased to grumble
about their injuries and even O'Leary mercifully kept
quiet, concentrating on watching the trail ahead. After
the first few minutes, Alcott was expecting to see
Lawson and the girl up ahead. The valley curved away
gently to the left at first, and patches of woodland
obscured the view in places. A few more minutes
passed before the valley opened up in front of them
and all four outlaws saw the two figures, over half a
mile ahead.

O'Leary let out a whoop of excitement and kicked

his horse into a full gallop.

'We can get them!' he yelled.

The other outlaws pushed their horses on too: the end of the long chase was in sight.

CHAPTER THIRTEEN

Although it was a relief to finally reach Lyons, Alec's mood was grim. He felt weak and a little light-headed after the gallop along the valley. The horses had, thankfully, kept the pace up well, but the outlaws had never been more than ten or fifteen minutes behind them. Somehow or another he was going to have to deal with them here, and he needed to find a solution pretty quickly. Alec quickly decided that their best chance of help lay in calling up a posse from around the Golden Nugget saloon. The guard at the nearby bank could also be called upon.

As Alec reined his horse to a halt, he heard his name called, in an unexpectedly familiar voice. Turning quickly in his saddle, a wave of dizziness blurred his vision for a few moments before he could properly recognize the aristocratic looking man hurrying along the sidewalk towards him.

'Karl!' he exclaimed in delight. 'What are you doing here?'

'We came to help you out,' his chief deputy replied, jumping down into the street.

Karl Firth was sometimes mistaken for the sheriff, instead of a deputy, which didn't surprise Alec. Karl was taller, handsome and, Alec felt, naturally more distinguished looking. His dark blond hair and crystal blue eyes seemed altogether more striking than Alec's own dark hair and eyes. Alec had long ago resigned himself to the belief that he would be overshadowed by his more colourful deputies.

'We got your telegram from Dronfield,' Karl explained. 'I wired Leadville to warn them that Alcott was probably in town. They wired back soon after to say there'd been no sign of him, so I thought I'd better let you know. I then wired Dronfield and they replied to tell me about your fight with Alcott and that you'd left town, with Alcott following soon after. I guessed you'd be heading this way so we came up on the train to help you.'

'I dinna care too much for the details right now,' Alec said, still grinning. 'I'm just glad you're here.'

'So am I,' Lacey interrupted. 'The sheriff's hurt.'

'Alec?' Karl's expression changed from pleasure to anxiety as he stepped closer to Alec's horse. He'd been standing on the opposite site to the wounded leg, and hadn't seen the blood that had soaked through bandages and trousers.

There were shouts of pleasure as Alec's other two deputies came running up. As they approached, Alec slid from his saddle, grateful for Karl's support through a wave of dizziness. Lacey found herself

149

approached by a handsome, dark-haired man with merry blue eyes, who grinned up at her.

'Miss Fry?' he said, holding out his hand. 'I'm Sam Liston, Alec's most trusted deputy. Let me help you down.'

Lacey had been mounting and dismounting her horse unaided for days now, but she couldn't resist Sam's boyish charm. She flushed slightly pink, and took his hand as she slid from her saddle.

Alec recovered from his dizziness and looked around. Ethan Oldfield had arrived too, slightly breathless and with a worried expression on his long face. His expression didn't worry Alec much, it was normal for Ethan, who played the role of pessimist as Sam played the role of clown. Both men were intelligent and loyal, and Alec was glad that all three of his deputies had quit the army at the same time he had, and continued to work with him.

'Ethan, take our horses,' Alec ordered. In spite of the dizziness, his mind had already been working on the forthcoming fight with Alcott. 'Miss Fry, please go into the bank over there and stay away from the door and windows.'

She looked at him anxiously. 'Take care, Sheriff.' When Alec nodded in reply, she hurried across the street.

Her words reminded Alec of something. He drew out his marshal's badge and pinned it to the front of his coat.

'You look pleased to be wearing that again,' Karl said.

Alec smiled. 'I am.' He glanced around at his deputies. 'I don't want a firefight on the main street; let's get ready to meet them as they come along the railroad.'

Sam grinned. 'We sure want to be ready for our guests when they arrive.'

The lawmen headed between buildings back to the railroad that ran along beside the town, Ethan hurrying to catch the others after hitching the horses. Alec limped, but kept up with the others. After a quick look about, he headed along the tracks towards the station. The others followed, confident that he had something in mind.

'Ethan, I want you over there.' Alec gestured to a shack on the far side of the tracks. 'Sam, at the ticket office. Karl and I will use this wagon as cover. I'll let them see me, so they come in past the ticket office and we'll be surrounding them.'

Ethan and Sam hurried off to their appointed places. Three men were waiting beside the ticket office and Alec sent Karl to move them, while he unhitched the heavy-legged horses from the empty buckboard wagon. He hurried them over to the group of men who were reluctantly leaving the ticket office.

'We don't want to miss the train,' one of them was protesting. 'It should be here any minute.'

'We'll hold it,' Alec said firmly. He handed the horses' reins to him. 'Take them through to the main street; I don't want them spooking or getting hurt when the shooting starts.'

This convinced the men more than Karl's warnings

had, and they hurried away. As the lawmen headed back to the wagon, Alec heard a new sound.

'I think the train's coming,' he warned.

'And Alcott too,' replied Karl, who had looked the other way.

The piercing whistle of the loco sounded as it approached the station in a sudden rush of sound and steam. The lawmen sprinted for the buckboard, Alec's injury forgotten in the tension. They scrambled aboard and climbed over into the back to use the seat as cover. Drawing his gun as he turned, Alec saw the loose group of four horsemen pounding along beside the tracks. As usual, the lanky figure of O'Leary, on his bay with its white face, was out in front.

'Stand and fight, you gutless law-dog!' O'Leary yelled, pulled his gun.

Alec stood up. 'Surrender. All of you drop your guns!' He bellowed in his best parade ground voice to be heard over the hissing and rumble of the train as it puffed to a halt alongside them, blowing off clouds of steam.

O'Leary let off a shot as he hauled his restless, blowing horse to a halt. It didn't come anywhere near close enough to worry Alec.

'Double on him,' Alec said, loosing off a shot that purposely came close to O'Leary without hitting him. He shifted sideways and dropped lower as Karl popped up and fired off a shot in turn.

More shots began to crash from around the station. Behind O'Leary, Houston had come under fire from Sam. Alcott and Hannigan had crossed the tracks to the other side of the train, where they were hidden from Alec and Karl. Gunfire from that direction suggested that Ethan had challenged them. Swirls of smoke and steam, from the locomotive and gun barrels, curled in the air. The smells of gunpowder, hot oil and metal were sharp in Alec's nose, after so many days out in the clear air of the mountains. O'Leary's horse whinnied as he fought it with legs and reins, to keep it facing the lawmen in the wagon.

He fired back, bellowing in frustration as the two lawmen took it in turns to take shots at him. O'Leary fired back frantically, his gun weaving around as his horse pranced beneath him. Alec fired, changed position as Karl fired, and fired again. One of O'Leary's shots hit the rear of the wagon seat, a few inches from where it covered him, making his pulse spike. Alec's mind stayed calm, in spite of the adrenaline running through him. He knew what he was doing and that the odds of O'Leary hitting either of them were small.

Then O'Leary pulled the trigger and nothing happened: he'd emptied his gun. It was the moment Alec had planned for. Both lawmen rose, aiming straight at the outlaw.

'Surrender!' Alec shouted. 'Drop your gun.'

O'Leary screamed and hurled his revolver in Alec's direction. Alec stayed dead still, as it flew past, a couple of feet from his left shoulder. As soon as it left his hand, O'Leary was bending in his saddle. He grabbed his rifle and began to haul it from its scabbard. Alec and Karl fired simultaneously and this time, neither man missed. O'Leary rocked in his saddle, dropping his hold of the rifle, and toppled sideways. He hit the ground, one foot still tangled in the stirrup. His bay bucked a couple of times, hoofs coming down onto the limp body, then it stood still, snorting. O'Leary hung from the stirrup, anchoring the anxious horse in place.

Alec and Karl scrambled down from the buckboard. A quick glance showed Alec that Houston was also on the ground, near the front wheels of the locomotive, Sam standing over him.

'What did you do to annoy him so bad?' Karl asked, indicating O'Leary as they cautiously approached the horse, guns still in hand.

'Stopped him from having his fun with Miss Fry, for one thing,' Alec replied. 'I think he had just one oar in the water though.'

Karl's reply was interrupted by a shout from the cab of the locomotive.

'Lawson, you two-faced skunk! Drop your gun!'

Alcott had hold of the driver, his revolver pressed against the man's head. The engineer was just visible behind them, his face fraught with helplessness. Alec halted, mentally cursing Alcott. He took a long breath.

'You can't get away,' he replied. 'Let the man go now.'

Alcott shook his head fiercely. 'I'm having this out with you now, Lawson. You killed Jacob, you killed Chuck, dammit. You're gonna pay for it. Both of you, drop your goddam guns now!'

From the corner of his eye, Alec saw Sam moving. He was crossing the tracks and going out of sight behind the locomotive. Alcott hadn't seen him, and so long as he kept looking at Alec, Sam could get around behind him without being noticed. Ethan was already there, though Alec didn't know if he'd been hurt in the shooting. It was Sam who had the best chance of bringing Alcott down though, for he had an uncanny knack with firearms. Alec had trusted his life to Sam's gun skills before, and was prepared to do so again. He just had to keep Alcott occupied while Sam got into position.

'I didn't mean for Jacob to die,' Alec said, fixing Alcott's gaze with his own.

'I don't damn well care!' Alcott's hand twitched and the driver gasped, his face drawn in fear. 'Don't make me tell you again, drop your guns, both of you.'

Karl bent and gently tossed his to land a few feet in front. Alec slowly followed suit, never taking his gaze from Alcott. The outlaw was on a knife edge, liable to act at any moment, and although his gun wasn't pointed at Alec, the sheriff felt horribly vulnerable. As he released his gun, he took a deep breath.

'It doesn't have to be like this,' he said, wondering whereabouts Sam was. 'You canna get away, Alcott, so why make it harder on yourself?'

'What have I got to lose?' Alcott hissed. Sweat was rolling down his face. 'Most likely I'll die, but I'll see you dead first.'

Alec's heart was pounding in his chest. He didn't know where Sam was, didn't know if he'd got a clear shot at Alcott. He did know that Sam wouldn't dare shoot while Alcott had his gun pressed to the driver's head, with the hammer cocked. He had to take the chance. Slowly, Alec raised his empty hands level with his shoulders.

'Go ahead then,' he said. 'Shoot me.'

Alcott's eyes widened for a moment, then narrowed as he focused. Alec saw the small movements, and as Alcott's hand moved, he was throwing himself sideways. A gun crashed, and for a few seconds Alec didn't know who'd fired. He landed, rolled and ended on his stomach, straining to see inside the cab. His leg hurt, but after the first moments, he knew it was the wound he'd already taken.

'Great shot,' Karl yelled.

The driver was standing by himself, gasping and shuddering. The sprawled form of Bill Alcott lay across the footplate, his head and one arm dangling over the edge. Blood dripped from his hair to the ground.

'It weren't so hard,' came Sam's drawl from the other side. 'Any crack shot could have done it.'

'Luckily for us, you managed it too,' Karl replied drily.

Alec grinned, happy to hear his deputies in their usual form. He tried to stand, but a wave of dizziness struck and he ended up sitting, his head bowed as his vision dimmed.

'Hey, careful there, Alec.'

He felt Karl beside him, supporting him as the greyness passed.

'I'm all right,' Alec insisted unconvincingly. He made no protest as Karl carefully helped him to stand.

'Hannigan?' Alec made the effort to call the question towards the locomotive.

'Down and done,' came back Ethan's reassuring answer from the other side. 'Alcott slipped aboard while I was busy with Hannigan.'

'Good.' Alec's voice faded as he swayed against Karl.

'Let's get you somewhere you can lie down,' Karl said. 'Sam and Ethan can take care of things here. You need to get that leg seen to before you bleed out, you stubborn, Scottish fool.'

'I've missed you, too,' Alec said sincerely.

'Alec? You have visitors.' Karl pushed open the door between the office at the front of the building, and the lawmen's quarters at the rear.

Alec placed the leather bookmark in the copy of *Treasure Island* he was reading and put the book on the small table beside his armchair. He'd spent the last two days in bed, which would normally have bored him, but he'd slept much of the time. He'd certainly appreciated the comfort of a mattress, a feather pillow, walls and a roof. There had also been the quiet nursing of Mrs Andersen, the comfortable middle-aged Swedish widow who had been taken on as housekeeper during the winter. Getting a house-keeper had been Alec's idea, and although they had been used to looking after themselves in the Army, it was good not to have to worry about cleaning, mending and laundry after a long day. Mrs Andersen had brought Alec tasty soup for his meals in bed and gently mothered him as he recovered. Lacey's aunt and uncle had paid a brief visit the day after his return home. They had thanked him profusely for taking care of their niece, and left a bottle of excellent Scotch in gratitude. Lacey and the dun horse returned with them to Leadville.

Now he was well enough to get dressed and come downstairs to sit in his wing-backed armchair. Alec's face lit up in a smile as he saw his visitors and he started to get to his feet.

'Oh, no, Sheriff. I'm sure you mustn't stand up,' Mrs Brown said firmly.

Alec gave in, not too reluctantly, and gestured to the other chairs. 'Please, come and join me. It's good to see ye, Mrs Brown, Lily.'

The two women joined him, but Alec's attention was almost entirely on the younger woman, Lily. The young, Chinese woman wore plain, unsophisticated clothes of muted colours, her black hair concealed beneath her bonnet. To Alec, the ordinary outfit made her delicate face, with the black, almond eyes, even more exotic and lovely. She smiled as she approached, and sat on one side of him, with Mrs Brown settling herself on the other.

'We're glad to have you back in town again, Sheriff,' Mrs Brown said. 'The Reverend Brown has been saying prayers for you in church.'

'I have been praying for you too,' Lily added, her voice soft. She spoke carefully, making the effort to articulate her words clearly, though she retained an accent.

'Thank you both,' Alec answered, smiling at each woman in turn.

158

Karl had returned to the offices, leaving the three alone.

'How are you?' Mrs Brown asked, looking at Alec's leg.

There was a bandage under his trousers, but luckily the wound had not got infected.

'I'm recovering well, thank you,' Alec replied. 'I'll not be very active for a while yet, but I should be walking around fine in a few days or so. How have you been getting on since I last saw you?' he asked Lily.

'I have been sewing,' she replied. 'I like sewing.'

'Lily is a natural with a needle,' Mrs Brown said. 'She keeps house quite nicely now, though she lacks experience of course. But she's a very neat sewer. I'm hoping she can get work sewing, or helping in a dry goods shop, later in the year.'

Alec let Mrs Brown do most of the talking: he was always happy to hear of Lily's new accomplishments. After the weeks with the outlaws, and the last few days riding through the mountains with Lacey, it was wonderful to be at home, quiet and relaxed for a little while. He was content just to sit and smile at Lily.

Settling back in his chair after the women left, Alec realized he was more tired than he'd thought. He needed to rest and recover for a while, but in a couple of days, he'd be strong enough for a short walk. He'd certainly be able to walk as far as the Browns' house, to call upon them, and Lily. This evening he would talk with Karl and the others about the work they were doing now, and what had happened during his time away, but for now. . . . Resting his head against the high back of his chair, Alec closed his eyes and began to doze.